TO PAINT A MURDER

A VERONICA HOWARD VINTAGE MYSTERY

E. J. GANDOLFO

outskirts
press

To Paint A Murder
A Veronica Howard Vintage Mystery
All Rights Reserved.
Copyright © 2019 E. J. Gandolfo
v4.0

This is a work of fiction. Names, characters, businesses, places, events, locales, and incidents are either the products of the author's imagination or used in a fictitious manner. Any resemblance to actual persons, living or dead, or actual events is purely coincidental.

The opinions expressed in this manuscript are solely the opinions of the author and do not represent the opinions or thoughts of the publisher. The author has represented and warranted full ownership and/or legal right to publish all the materials in this book.

This book may not be reproduced, transmitted, or stored in whole or in part by any means, including graphic, electronic, or mechanical without the express written consent of the publisher except in the case of brief quotations embodied in critical articles and reviews.

Outskirts Press, Inc.
http://www.outskirtspress.com

Paperback ISBN: 978-1-9772-0311-3

Cover Photo © 2019 www.gettyimages.com. Author Photo: Shari Nichols Photography. All rights reserved - used with permission.

Outskirts Press and the "OP" logo are trademarks belonging to Outskirts Press, Inc.

PRINTED IN THE UNITED STATES OF AMERICA

For Fr. Ken Gandolfo, brother, friend, and spiritual compass

A special thank you to my friend Jerome Curley, fellow author and technical consultant; and to Lieutenant Thomas Reddy, Lynn, MA. Police Department for advice on police procedures.

"I'm always satisfied with the best."
Oscar Wilde

PROLOGUE

It always gives him great pleasure to look around the room, to savor the sheer beauty of it and its contents. At a glance, it is a beautifully decorated library furnished with an oxblood leather tufted sofa and matching chair and ottoman. However, this room also contains an antique desk rumored to have once belonged to a long dead French king. On the desk rests a pair of nineteenth-century silver and enamel inkwells from the Fabergé workrooms and a jeweled picture frame from the collection of a fabled Greek shipping family. The woodwork and crown moldings are custom carved of the finest mahogany and the parquet floor beneath the palace-sized oriental carpet is polished to a high gloss finish.

He smiles as he remembers driving the decorator to distraction while agonizing over the color of the wall paint. "It has to be just right," he complained. "The color must be the proper foil for the pictures that will be hung—not too dark and not too light." In the end, he got his way...as usual. His money and name always smooth away problems.

Almost as important as the wall color and decor is the door. It slides back and forth noiselessly and is specially designed for the room, not just to ensure privacy but for retaining optimal temperature settings. The trompe l'oeil pattern facing the outside corridor determines that no one will ever know the room exists, and the secret latch that triggers the open-close mechanism is known only to him.

For this room is a museum. If he had to insure the collection of oil paintings currently hanging on the walls, the estimate would be in the several millions of dollars. After all, he is a connoisseur, a collector, an art expert. No amount of money is too much for him to spend on his passion.

He employs an agent to scour auction rooms and comb catalogue sales for the pictures he wants. When the bidding paddle goes up, his name is kept out of the transaction, and he wants it that way. He needs to be anonymous at any cost because the bulk of his art collection is stolen. Yes, he peppers his acquisitions with legitimate purchases, but he knows full well that the paintings that give him the greatest pleasure are the ones he steals.

Sliding the key he keeps on his person at all times in the lock, he opens the desk drawer, carefully removes a leather-bound book that catalogues his collection in code, and reaches to pour a glass of brandy. He sips contentedly, knowing he has more paintings hidden than some museums have on display. His arrogant laugh echoes around the room. *Let those imbeciles race around trying to catch me while I sit here in my own private little world. Isn't it heartwarming to have a hobby!*

CHAPTER 1

The morning began as forecasted, heavy rain and cool. It was unseasonable weather for Boston in early June, and Veronica Howard's mood matched her surroundings. The daily walk to work down Commonwealth Avenue usually helped clear the cobwebs, but today it seemed that she could only focus on the magnolia trees that fronted Back Bay's beautiful old brownstones and the wilting flowers they deposited on the wet and uneven brick pavement, making walking slippery and hazardous.

She did her best thinking during her morning walk. Today her mind was swirling with ideas for the advertising campaign she was working on. As head copywriter at Acme Advertising Agency, she took her hard-earned position seriously. She was preoccupied with deadlines and coordinating with the art department for an afternoon client conference. The corner traffic light turned green through her transparent plastic umbrella, and she crossed the street.

Her daily routine was usually much the same. Breakfast consisted of two cups of black coffee and, depending on how indulgent she felt, a sweet roll. She hardly ever worried about putting on weight and silently thanked her parents for the genes she inherited. She loved to eat, and even though she lived alone in a small, one-bedroom apartment, she always took time to prepare meals in her miniscule galley kitchen and serve herself on pieces from her collection of old blue and white china. She showered and dressed carefully from her overstuffed closet of vintage clothing. Her unique style of dressing was her trademark.

It could be said she was one of those women who could put her finger on anything at a moment's notice. Her closet was arranged by color with shoes and handbags neatly lined up according to the seasons. There wasn't much closet space in her apartment, but she was able to use her organizational skills to figure out how to keep things neat and accessible.

Veronica Howard had nothing to complain about on this rainy morning except that she was bored. She bored easily and wondered once again whether her life wasn't getting stagnant. She had a good job, a boyfriend who cared about her, and good health. She was popular, successful, competent, and it helped that she was considered attractive; a middle-aged woman blessed with good legs and a slim figure. Her shiny, black hair was abundant, and she wore it cut in a fashionable bob. Her cat-green eyes reflected intelligence and wit. Yes, there really wasn't much to complain about, but still, she was bored.

Acme Advertising was a midsized agency employing over fifty people. She had worked for them for about fourteen years, rising from the secretarial pool to her current position as chief copywriter. She always knew she possessed a talent for writing and wanted to progress from typing other people's work to creating her own, but the opportunity to show her ability never seemed to present itself.

One day, a break came in the form of a looming deadline. A rampant case of the flu had disabled several members of the copy department, and her boss, who was aware of her desire to write, suggested Veronica as a last-minute replacement. She was asked how women might react to a new product line from the account, a major ladies underwear manufacturer. Never shy about offering her opinion, she was encouraged to put her suggestions in a proposal that was met with enthusiasm by the client. The resulting campaign was a great success, and her promotion and new job title promptly followed. Over the years, she advanced through the ranks to a comfortable position at the agency. Her organizational skills and ability to focus on her job never let her down and the competitive nature of the advertising business kept her on her toes.

Being part of a team fed her desire to create and enhance, but she was always perfectly happy to work on her own. She loved her job, but after several years, her enthusiasm for touting toothpaste, lip gloss, and pet food began to wane. Her real love was antiques and vintage clothing, and her long-range plan was to retire early and finally have time to pursue her passion full time. She spent weekends going to yard sales, flea markets, and thrift shops. Antique shows called to her like a siren's song. She loved to dress in vintage clothing and recognized that the workmanship and beautiful fabrics said as much about her taste as did other women who insisted on wearing outfits with multiple designers' logos.

Veronica's unique style was also reflected in the way she furnished her apartment in a turn-of-the-century brownstone located on a quiet side street, a short distance to the Charles River. The living room was painted a pale yellow that made the fourteen-foot ceilings appear even higher. A large, 1930s tufted sofa covered in cream silk dominated the room. Two ornamental glass orbs tied with silk tassels decorated the arms. A matching chair and ottoman gave a glamorous, vintage, movie star look to the room. She draped antique shawls across two lamps to diffuse the light and add drama, and the gilt wood Art Deco cocktail table had a glass top that reflected the liquor bottles arranged on it. A cut glass champagne bucket rested on a silver-plated pedestal, and a six-foot modern brass sculpture stood sentry at the front door.

The small bedroom also reflected her love of vintage items. The bedspread was powder-pink satin with matching pillow covers. A dressing table, purchased at an estate sale, housed her collection of antique perfume bottles, and the Victorian cheval mirror in ornamental iron stood in a corner next to a shelf lined with old compacts and vintage purses. The neighborhood was an old established one not populated with student housing as so much of the Back Bay was these days. It was unusual to hear noises that were not the expected big-city sounds, and she was glad of it.

She walked home after a particularly busy day at the agency and stopped to collect her mail from the downstairs entry hall. There were five other apartments in her building and all the occupants worked during the day except for the superintendent, who had the whole basement apartment to himself. He was a kindly man who always stopped to chat with Veronica when he saw her.

"How's the wonderful world of advertising today, Miss Howard?" his usual question, as he handed her a collection of letters and circulars. "Did you happen to hear the commotion outside last night around midnight?"

"Now that you mention it, Mr. Bello, I did hear loud noises late last night. Any problems I should know about?"

He relished gossip, and now he had a willing audience. Scratching his beard and leaning against the hall table, he began.

"The police came around earlier this morning asking if I had noticed anything out of the ordinary. Seems someone reported a man lying on the sidewalk one street over with multiple stab wounds. They think he may have been connected with a big art theft that took place last night."

"Wow," she said. "This has always been such a quiet neighborhood. Were you able to tell them anything?"

"Well, you know at my age, the old kidneys flare up now and then, so I was able to tell them I heard running footsteps past my bathroom window around midnight. Living below street level, I was able to see a pair of black sneakers with orange stripes on the side, and the cops seemed happy with that information. The noise you heard was probably the squad car with sirens blaring."

Veronica laughed. "I know it's not funny, but that's just the background noise of living in the city. But still, it makes you stop to wonder what painting is worth a man's life."

CHAPTER 2

Veronica arrived at the office slightly wet despite the coverage of her large umbrella and vintage Burberry raincoat. She liked to reach her desk before the rest of the department, start the coffee machine, and enjoy the aroma and taste of the first cup in solitude. Her routine was to peruse the newspapers for her clients' ads, and this morning, she noted the headlines first. Lately, there seemed to be quite a few stolen artworks stories, and she made a mental note to mention them to Harry, her boyfriend, an avid art collector. Her coworkers started to drift in, and the friendly camaraderie of office routine took her away from her reverie.

Lately, a rumor had been going around that Acme Advertising was engaged in buy-out talks with Styles & Company, a large and flashy competitor who employed a predominantly young staff. It was well known they were driven by perks of big bonus money and long expense account lunches that Acme rarely offered their employees except to the occupants of executive row. If it came to it, she was torn between staying at her job for another few years or handing in her notice. Advertising was lately becoming a younger person's game. Her secret wish had always been to open a vintage clothing shop and fill it with antiques and unique items. Perhaps fate would decide for her.

That afternoon, the rumor was confirmed, and the Styles human resources manager made it clear that Veronica's loyalty to the old firm would never be rewarded in the new regime. It seemed that middle-aged copywriters were not on their agenda, no matter how talented and chic they were.

Her best friend at the agency, Amanda, an account executive, was asked to stay at her job. Several years younger than Veronica, she knew how to navigate the choppy waters of corporate politics. Unlike her friend, she decided that her career path was going to be with Styles. Lunch that day was depressing as they ate at their usual busy and noisy health food restaurant.

"I'm sorry, Ronnie, but I have to stay put. Old Man Styles offered me a nice raise and a chance to front the newest account."

"Is it worth putting up with his leers and innuendoes about delving in and working late at the office?" she asked, eyeing the lentil salad platter going by.

"Don't worry about me; I can handle him. I'm just worried about you and what you'll be doing for a salary. I hear the Patterson Agency is looking for good people. Why don't you apply?" Looking over the menu, she asked, "What looks good?"

"Mango smoothie. You know, they're doing me a favor. With some of the money Aunt Gillian left me, I just might open my own antique shop. You know I've always wanted to do that. So maybe now is the right time."

"A store sounds like an awful lot of work. What the devil is in a nut burger?"

"Nuts. I'll be my own boss, and that sounds very attractive to me right now," said Veronica, warming to the idea. "And," she continued, "if worse comes to worse, Harry will always help me out with the details. He can always find the time to take out of his busy schedule of racquetball at the club and dinner parties with mummy and daddy."

"I'll miss you, Ronnie. You always seem to know what you want. And even if Harry is as dull as ditch water, at least you know you can always count on him in a pinch. Herbal tea?"

"I'd prefer a gin and tonic, but, yes, let's order herbal tea. Actually, I'd give my right arm for a hot fudge sundae right now."

Across town, another lunch was taking place. The setting was very different and health food was not on the menu. The exclusive men's club was founded at the turn of the last century and was only open to members who were vetted by their peers. To the casual observer, the gray sandstone building with a discreet brass plate on the ornamental iron front gate bore only the legend, "Members Only," having no other identification. A uniformed porter sat inside the front door gently nodding to those august personages lucky enough to gain admittance. The heavily carpeted entry hall contained portraits of the late Victorian-era captains of industry that founded the place. The tasteful chandeliers provided muted lighting, and the faint clinking of cutlery from the dining room could be heard by the members only if they strained their hearing.

Today, a table by one of the windows overlooking the enclosed garden of willow trees and shrubbery was occupied by two men dressed like all the others in the room in custom-made, three-piece suits. Their whispered conversation was interrupted by a uniformed waiter delivering their drinks order on a silver platter. Rain was still falling at a steady pace outside while they calmly discussed how to murder a business associate.

CHAPTER 3

Harrison Thornhill Hunt, III, Veronica's boyfriend of three years, lived in his family's ancestral mansion on Beacon Hill, Boston's most upscale neighborhood, long the home of the storied Brahmins, those movers and shakers whose wealth and influence could be traced back to their colonial ancestors. Harry's Andover prep school and Harvard education choices followed the usual path expected of sons of old money.

His amiable personality and nonchalant air made him popular with his peers, and his habit of wearing three-piece suits even on the most humid of days blended well with his prep school friends whose haberdashery choices ran along the same lines. Polished cordovan leather shoes, plain carat gold cuff links, and tailored suits from the classic shops along Newbury Street were the styles that were never deviated from. A Burberry raincoat, a cashmere overcoat, two handmade tuxedos, several shirts with discreet pinstripes, and silk ties from Hermès rounded out his wardrobe. The car of choice was a Porsche sports model in black, and his grandfather's Patek Philippe gold wristwatch was worn alternated with his father's Rolex on special occasions.

He was a man who didn't need to work for a living. He possessed a sharp mind and quiet manner and was used to the respect of his peers. His family money and position ensured financial independence. Harry had never married and was adept at sidestepping serious relationships. He liked being a popular man about town and was never at a loss for invitations. His crowd included several former debutantes who were board members of charities, museums, and social welfare organizations. He could dance, play tennis, make polite and witty conversation, drink without going overboard, and could always be relied on to make a healthy donation to whatever cause he attended.

The family vacation home on Cape Cod is where he kept his boat, a classic affair with twin outboard motors. He was a member of the yacht club board and attended all their summer functions, and his golf membership at the country club was a long-standing one. The women he dated were the daughters of his parents' friends who were usually between husbands.

Harry met Veronica when she was assigned to create copy for his family's business. They owned textile mills and shoe tanneries that previous generations started and formed the basis for many old guard Yankee fortunes. These days when diversification was key, banking and insurance guaranteed that future generations would enjoy the same prosperity.

The insurance account was a large one for Acme Advertising and represented a major cash flow for the agency. The campaign centered around a television and print schedule, and Veronica attended several client meetings as head copywriter. The presentation was well thought out, and Harry noted that Veronica had her own mind and ideas and wasn't afraid to argue her position. He also didn't fail to notice her long legs and manicured crimson toes encased in high heels either and was instantly smitten.

Suddenly, he decided to become more involved with the nuts and bolts of the campaign and suggested drinks and dinner to go over her suggestions. He was smirking when he asked her, and Veronica thought she would have to spend the evening avoiding unwanted advances. *After all, I can't really refuse the invitation because he is the client*, she thought. The meeting at the agency went on past business hours, and Harry suggested they dine at a popular hotel located next door to the agency. They walked over, and she caught him looking her up and down appreciatively as they entered the bar area.

Veronica had to admit that he wasn't bad looking in spite of his dressing in a rather preppy style. He exuded an air of confidence and quiet intelligence which was not lost on her. They sat at the bar which was a popular meeting place for the after-work crowd and was starting to fill up. They made small talk, and she discovered he had a rather quirky sense of humor. Once or twice she caught him looking at her legs, and she was flattered in spite of her initial reservation. When their table was ready, the head waiter greeted Harry by name and inquired after his health.

They placed their orders and proceeded to discuss the advertising campaign, but after a few minutes, he changed the subject. She intrigued him, and he found himself wanting to know everything about this woman. He asked if she was wearing Chanel No. 5 perfume, and she smiled and nodded yes. They spoke of their hobbies, and he learned of her fondness for vintage clothing and antique furniture and her wish to someday open her own store. Her clarity of thought was very sexy to him, and the way she dressed and presented herself was, he had to admit, altogether different from the bland and drab society girls he usually dated. He appreciated the way her mind worked, and he very much liked the way she looked.

She found herself smiling a lot and approved of his quiet confidence. He served on several boards of local charities and spoke with particular passion about the need for more volunteers at the local food bank. In spite of herself, she offered to help and told him she would also speak to the agency principals about underwriting a program for the group. Harry also hinted at one point that he was a silent investor in several business ventures but elaborated no further.

After dinner, Harry suggested a brandy in the lounge. A popular jazz group was appearing for a limited engagement, and the room was full. A good table up front magically appeared for Harry, and they found themselves totally involved in the music. During a break, they realized that jazz was another thing they had in common. All talk of business was abandoned, and Veronica was trying to figure how to ask Harry if he was ever married. She had just decided in her mind to ask Mandy when he blurted out the same question to her. She explained that she had come close once or twice but considered herself lucky to have escaped. He laughed and agreed and admitted to the same. They gazed at each other with a new understanding. She asked him to call her Ronnie.

Her past love affairs mostly revolved around the men's ardor and her eventual boredom. The men she usually dated were in the advertising business as well, even though she saw them as cookie-cutter types affecting Madison Avenue's version of style. They wore tassel loafers, Armani aftershave, and pasted on smiles. She supposed they had their jobs in common but usually, little else. None were serious suitors, and none were big passions, and she seemed always to be in a permanent state of waiting for that special someone. She always thought she would recognize him when he came along but was never quite sure if the promise of him would match up to the actual man standing in front of her.

Veronica wanted a companion but realized early on that she was more career-minded than marriage-minded. Longing for a husband and children just wasn't her style. When she met Harry, she became aware that he felt the same. If their relationship flourished because of it, then so much the better.

The next morning, a beautiful arrangement of summer flowers from Boston's premier florist was delivered to her desk. The card thanked her for a lovely evening, and everyone who passed by asked if it was her birthday. The blush was still on her face when the phone rang, and Harry was asking her if she was free for lunch. She happily accepted, and they started dating regularly after that. Both had realized that they had found in each other the different and special relationship they were looking for.

One day, the human resource manager stopped by her desk and suggested she come to his office for a short conference. He asked her point-blank if the gossip he had heard was true about her and Harry. He explained it was company policy that dating clients was strictly frowned upon. She couldn't deny what he already knew and assured him that the account would not be compromised if they continued to see each other socially. The man did not back down and told her that her job would be in immediate jeopardy if she continued.

That night she told Harry about the scene and he was livid. Next day, he called one of the partners and threatened to pull his account if Veronica was in any way embarrassed or put on the spot again. The manager received a stern dressing-down, and the incident was never mentioned again. She had found her knight in shining armor.

About a month before the Styles takeover, one of Veronica's cosmetic clients, Glamour Puff, decided to launch a new product line. She suggested a major presentation at a cocktail party using a vintage disco theme. The idea was met with great enthusiasm, and she took over the organizing of the party. It would be a fitting end to her advertising career as well.

The event was to be held at the newly built Waterfront Hotel on the wharf in one of their large function rooms overlooking the harbor. In the spirit of the theme, she arranged for a mirrored revolving disco ball to be installed and hired professional models to circulate wearing short, sequined dresses from the era while distributing complimentary Glamour Puff products. The music was loud and pulsating and put everyone in a party mood. The local television stations covered the impromptu fashion show, while many celebrities took advantage of photo opportunities.

She had always looked forward to the social aspects of her job, and this evening was to be the end of her successful career. She dressed carefully and chose a chic vintage minidress covered in navy blue and silver sequins sewn in a fringe that shimmered in the light as she moved.

It was the perfect night for a party. The weather was warm with a slight breeze, and the distant lights from the moored yachts in the harbor twinkled and reflected on the window walls of the room. The five-piece band played popular songs from the era alternating with a disc jockey who did the same. She circulated in the crowd while the waiters passed trays of canapés and champagne. Many were aware this was her last client event and congratulated her and wished her good luck.

Before she had left the office to go to the hotel to check on arrangements, Harry called and apologized for not being able to meet her after the party as planned. A last-minute appointment had come up that he couldn't get out of, but he promised to call her in the morning. He wished her the best and hung up.

A large crowd had gathered at the bar talking shop, and she was feeling nostalgic. Compliments and a few drinks, plus the heat and noise from the tightly packed room was giving her a headache, so she excused herself for a breath of fresh air. She headed to the ladies' room when she happened to see two men, one looking exactly like Harry, entering the elevator. *How odd*, she thought. *Maybe his appointment is at the hotel, but if that is true, he would have mentioned it as he knew I was here tonight. Oh well, I'll remember to ask him about it tomorrow.*

When Harry called the next morning to ask how the party went, she told him she had seen him at the hotel talking to another man.

"I must have a double," he laughed. "They say we all do. It couldn't have been me you saw because I was across town in Cambridge at an alumni meeting that lasted too long, as usual."

I must have been mistaken, she thought. *It was hot in there, and I did have a few drinks. Maybe I need to wear my harlequin glasses more often.*

Her retirement party was well attended, and the parting gifts were a mixture of kitschy knickknacks, soppy greeting cards, and a potted plant. *Not much to show for fourteen years of work*, she thought. Mandy gave her a gift card to her favorite department store and promised to call her for lunch. As she was placing her belongings in a cardboard box, she realized her long-delayed decision to leave, prompted by the new management's mandate, was a mixed blessing. She was giving up the safety net of a steady job, even if it was one she had grown tired of, and looked at it as the impetus she needed to open her shop.

Maybe now life will offer a little more excitement, she thought, getting in to the elevator for the last time. *It seems I've always played it safe. Maybe my new venture will give me a taste for the exotic, the unusual, the dangerous...*

She laughed out loud at herself in the empty elevator. *Who do you think you are, Veronica Howard*, she thought, *Mata Hari?*

At about the same time a dubious business meeting was taking place across town in a dilapidated warehouse on the wharf that usually doubled as a fish-processing plant. Today, it was empty except for the pile of nets needing mending and broken lobster traps piled in one corner with plastic buckets used to catch the gutted entrails of fish. Upstairs, two well-dressed men in business suits looking decidedly out of place were sitting at a table while two were standing. One roughly dressed man with a scowl on his face wearing work boots and a plaid shirt was holding up a man bleeding from a wound on his forehead who couldn't remain upright on his own.

"I'm asking you once again, what did you do with the truck?" said the younger suit, addressing his remarks to the injured one. The question was met with silence, so he nodded to the other whose fist flew out and landed another blow to the side of his captive's head. He staggered, doubled over, and fell with a thud on the floor.

"We're not going to get any more out of him," sneered the workman.

"You give up too easily," said the suit. "He needs to be reminded once again that memory loss is not an option."

A groan escaped from the fallen prisoner. He was hauled to his feet once more, shoved in a chair, and given a drink from the bottle of whiskey on the table. They waited in silence as he gulped down several swallows.

"I told you before," he whispered, "I was ambushed trying to make the drop. They pulled me out of my seat, hit me over the head, and when I woke up, the truck was gone." Three pairs of eyes bored into him.

As he reached for the bottle again, the younger man leaned over and grabbed his arm. "Do you *really* expect us to believe you? No one else knew about the robbery, and we took extra precautions by moving the date forward."

"I don't know nothin' about that. I just did what I was told, like I always do. Someone found out, attacked me, and stole the shipment."

The older suit stood up, walked over to the prisoner, put his face a few inches from his, and shouted, "Those paintings are worth three-quarters of a million, and I want them back!"

"Look, you gotta believe me," he whined. "There's a

leak somewhere, but it's not me. I need the money you pay, and you know you can trust me. I don't wanna go back to the joint." He reached for the bottle again. "I'm not gonna double-cross you."

They were all silent for a while. Finally, the older man sighed as he drummed his manicured fingernails on the table. He turned to the others. "We can't let this temporary setback ruin our long-range plans. We'll find out who did this, and they *will* pay the price. Make no mistake about it; they *will* pay." He stood up, and the meeting was over.

CHAPTER 4

Veronica thought she would like to open her store on the North Shore. Located within an easy commuting distance from her apartment in Boston, the towns and cities of historical significance had always appealed to her, especially those near the ocean. She was always fascinated by nineteenth-century American history when clipper ships sailed from the ports of Salem, Newburyport, and New Bedford trading with China and the great ships that brought back whale ivories and oils, important commodities in their day.

On her days off, she would drive to the old piers, breathe in the salt air, and close her eyes and picture what it must have been like to trade with countries across the globe. New England antique shops still carried the beautiful hand painted Rose Medallion and Canton porcelain that were so plentiful during the China Trade that they were used as ballast in the ships. Aunt Gillian would take her to museums when she was a child to see these wonderful treasures. She fell in love with the exotic furniture inlaid with mother of pearl, the fabulous silk robes of the mandarins where the embroidery was so fine that needle workers would eventually go blind from stitching them, and the dark paintings of the clipper ships that told the story of the East India Company trade.

The romance of the sea was special to her, and she eventually found the perfect site for her shop in Bromfield, a small town about twelve miles north of Boston on the coast. She called Mandy and described a cozy shop located on a street aptly named Posy Place. She fell in love with the front bow window that looked like it had come from a Dickens novel. The developers wanted to recreate a Victorian English high street, so they cobblestoned the street and sidewalks and erected old-fashioned street lamps. The look was enchanting. Next door was a quaint flower shop with a pink awning, and down the street was a bakery that had a small outdoor cafe that they set up in warm weather. The delicious odors of freshly baked bread wafted invitingly, and the street generated a lot of foot traffic. She couldn't wait to sign the lease.

She called Harry who was pressed into service to paint, wash windows, and commission a sign for the new venture.

"So what's the name of this place going to be?" he asked, sweeping the floor.

"I was thinking of something along the lines of "Veronica's Vintage," she said.

He started to laugh. "And I thought you were an ideas person. That name sounds like something from another century."

"That's the point, Harry. I want people to shop here and expect to find genuine antiques and vintage items, not the stuff that was made overseas yesterday."

"Okay, but where are you going to find the things you want to sell?"

"In case you haven't noticed, my apartment is loaded with items I couldn't say no to, and there's even more in Aunt Gillian's garage that we need to clean out and bring back here."

"What's with the 'we'? I can only fit so much in my Porsche."

"Guess I'll just have to find another boyfriend with a bigger car," she laughed, carrying several hat boxes over to the counter.

"You know, Veronica, I think your natural curiosity about things is really behind this idea of opening a shop. You've always been nosy about people and things, and you never seem to be able to pass up a good mystery, even if there isn't one."

"That's all part of my charm." She winked, and he leaned over to kiss her cheek.

She was happy Harry was supportive of her enthusiasm to open the shop. She knew she could confide in him, and if he thought her idea wasn't a good one, he would tell her. His good, solid advice rarely disappointed her. It could be said that Harry was the strong, silent type of man. He reminded her of a happy golden retriever, with his straw-colored hair, pale and intelligent blue eyes, and easy, lopsided grin.

She was fond of Harry, but she wasn't head over heels in love with him. He was a popular extra man at Beacon

Hill parties, and once in a while, she would accompany him. She sometimes found it hard to hide her bored expression while listening to his friends talk about their troubles finding a nanny or complaining about their trips to Tahiti and Micronesia. She knew she could never compete with his crowd but happily accepted invitations to the ballet and symphony on whose board of directors he sat, all the while knowing his participation was as much a family and ancestral obligation as pleasure.

Veronica often wondered what his friends and family thought of her. Oh, they were always pleasant and civil when they met her, but she couldn't help but wonder if she measured up to their standards. But Harry had made his choice, and he often told her how proud he was of her accomplishments, pointing out that her very individual way of dressing and thinking was what set her apart from the women he had usually dated. It was some time after they had started dating exclusively that she told him about her family.

Veronica was orphaned after losing both parents in a tragic car crash when she was a young girl. An only child, she was brought up by her father's sister, her aunt Gillian, who took her to live in her large Victorian house.

Gillian was a spinster and free spirit who had always wanted a family but not necessarily the husband one needed in those days to accomplish the task. When she became guardian, she indulged the girl and developed her love of vintage clothing and antiques by surrounding her with the beautiful objects she collected. Her attic overflowed with trunks and bureaus filled with every conceivable kind of collectible, and it was a treasure hunt for Veronica to go through the drawers and pull out her aunt's wonderful relics from another era.

There were ostrich feather and sequined fans stored in their long, velvet-lined boxes; evening bags of enameled mesh metal that looked like little oriental carpets; lace and satin camisoles in lovely pastel colors of peach, cream, and powder blue, all folded and in their original tissue paper. Lots of powder compacts, some on thin chains with attached lipstick tubes were in the drawers, along with satin gloves in every length from wrist to elbow, and shoes.

The shoe collection alone took up one wall of the attic. Satin slippers with Louis heels, T-strap shoes in soft, buttery suede, and even a pair that matched a fan, all neatly arranged in boxes. Hat boxes were stacked on top of the bureaus, and their contents revealed huge cartwheel brimmed hats with elaborate decorations. There was even a hat with a whole stuffed blackbird with iridescent wings perched on one side. There were cloche hats in wool felt in every color of the spectrum and brimmed hats with netting attached. Veronica particularly liked a small black crown affair sewn with large paste stones that sat on the back of her head. She gazed in the mirror on the wall arranging the net veil rakishly over one eye and posed in a model's stance that made Gillian laugh.

Porcelain containers of hat pins were clustered on

bureau tops; their long metal stems topped with glass rhinestones of every color and form, looking like little jewels even in the dim light of the attic lamps. The large wardrobes were stuffed with dresses, and the more fragile pieces were boxed and neatly labeled and stacked beside the shoes.

Gillian's beloved tuxedo cat, Fiona, usually accompanied them to the attic. She liked to perch on a rocking chair and watch the proceedings. Whenever she spotted a feather, she leaped off and tried to swipe it with her paw. When she was convinced the effort wasn't worth it, she returned to her velvet pillow to resume her nap. Veronica would take the opportunity to drape her with a rhinestone necklace, and they would laugh when the shiny objects whipped her into a frenzy again.

One rainy afternoon, Veronica came across an old photo of a glamorous woman with Marcel-waved hair and bee-stung lips wearing a glittery, beaded chemise dress and clutching a long cigarette holder.

"Who is this?" she asked, holding the photo up so Gillian could see.

"Actually, Veronica, it's me. You may not believe it, but I didn't just collect all these clothes. I wore them."

She took another look at the photo of the flapper in the come-hither pose and laughed. "I already guessed you liked to go out because of your extensive wardrobe. Wow, you must have been quite a heartbreaker in your day!"

"Yes," said Gillian, matter-of-factly. "I had a number of beaus, but none of them captured my heart completely."

She glanced at the photo again, a small smile of remembrance on her lips.

"Now I have you to reminisce with and relive my youth once again. I love you as if you were my own daughter, and I really don't miss my past at all."

The two women hugged. "And I love you back, Aunt Gillian. You and your red lipstick, great vintage collection, and wonderful stories."

When her aunt passed away in her 90s, Veronica was orphaned once again. Gillian left her the house, all the furnishings and contents, and a substantial stock portfolio. It seemed that one of her former admirers advised her to read the *Wall Street Journal* on a daily basis, and she bought some solid stocks that were enough of a legacy to finance her beloved niece's dream of opening her own vintage shop.

CHAPTER 5

Late spring turned into summer and Veronica's Vintage was ready to open for business. Judicious advertising, word of mouth, and nagging all her friends to shop resulted in a profitable month. The store was packed with lovely inlaid furniture, some of Aunt Gillian's cut glass and hand painted porcelain, old silver, and lots of vintage costume jewelry.

The area dedicated to vintage clothing was especially popular with college students and young mothers. They enjoyed going through the racks of dresses from the 1970s and 1980s, and their mothers fondly remembered the fashion for poodle skirts and penny loafers from the 1950-'60s. The bright, vivid colors of the beat generation contrasted sharply with the paper-white linens worn in the Victorian era that featured hand pleated tops, smocking, and bustle skirts. The 1920s were well represented with chemise dresses and button-down blouses of pastel silk. The hat displays always elicited giggles, and the shoes and vintage boots were especially in demand with the younger customers.

The jewelry counter was always busy, and Veronica kept it well stocked with customer favorites of bright and sparkling rhinestones, rope necklaces of chains and pearls, chandelier earrings, large pins in the forms of butterflies and animal motifs, and bracelets of all kinds.

Word of mouth about Bromfield's newest shop prompted several customers to bring in their vintage items to sell. She was in her element, and the receipts from the first month's business told her she had made the right decision to open her store.

Once in a while, Veronica would dress in some of the clothing she sold, her slim figure making the most of the styles from an earlier era. She was her own best advertisement, and her friendly and easy manner made her a popular merchant in the area. Even the local traffic cop, Officer Joe Banks, took his coffee breaks at the shop, often bringing freshly made croissants and latte from the bakery down the street to share when Veronica wasn't busy helping customers.

Joe was a roly-poly man with a florid complexion and a ready smile. He had been on the beat for several years and knew all the shop owners by name; he was as much a goodwill ambassador for the area as a law enforcement officer. She looked forward to chatting with him and listened for the bell over the door each morning. Today, he walked in with coffee and Danish pastry.

"Mighty kind of you, Joe. I can really use the caffeine this morning. What's going on in the neighborhood?"

He sat down on a Windsor chair and spread a napkin on his lap. "Don't mean to scare you, Ronnie, but there was a break-in at the pawn shop a few streets over last night. The guys at the station said they entered by the back door and forced the locks. I've been after the owner to install an updated alarm system for years. Now, I think he finally got the message."

"What did they take?" she asked, munching on a pastry.

"That's the odd part about it," he said, wiping strawberry jam from his mouth with the napkin. "Nothing seems to be missing, but they tossed the place pretty good. Threw things around looking for whatever. I mean, there must be plenty of valuables to steal in a pawn shop."

She promised to review her store insurance policy and had Joe check her locks. Out of curiosity, she decided to walk over to the pawn shop later that day. The owner was talking to a uniformed policeman with a notepad.

"I just don't understand it because nothing seems to be missing," said the owner, scratching his head. "Don't get me wrong. I'm thrilled about that, but what the hell were they looking for?" Veronica introduced herself and was cautioned by both men to be vigilant at her shop.

While they were talking, a woman in a red knit hat with a small brim pulled down over one eye entered the store. The owner excused himself and asked, "May I help you?"

"Just looking for gift ideas," she said and walked to the rear of the store.

Veronica decided to look around at the eclectic merchandise for sale. Stacks of guitars were leaning against a wall under a shelf display of miscellaneous electric appliances, radios, and televisions. Everything seemed dusty and in disarray. Stacks of video games and CDs took up a table, and there was a wire cage around a desk with a safe behind it.

Lots of junk here, she thought, and as she started to walk out the door, she saw a crumpled piece of paper on the floor. Not really thinking about it, she automatically stooped to pick it up and looked around for a trash can. The cop warned her again about keeping her guard up. She absentmindedly nodded while shoving the paper in her coat pocket and left the store.

The woman in the hat followed her out the door and back to her shop. As she took off her coat and hung it up on the rack by her desk at the rear of the store, the woman spoke up.

"I couldn't help overhearing about the robbery down the street just now," she said. "You have to be so careful these days."

"I couldn't agree with you more. Is there something special you're looking for?"

"I really love vintage clothing," she said, fingering an embroidered shawl. "Is this silk?" she asked, taking it off the manikin.

"Yes, it's turn of the century and was displayed on my late aunt's piano. There is another down here in different colors," said Veronica, walking to the center of the store. She turned around, but there was no one there. The shawl was on the floor, and the door that led to the back alley was wide open.

She ran to the door and looked out, but the woman was nowhere in sight. As she walked back inside, she noticed her coat was on the floor. She stooped to pick it up and saw that the pocket was turned out, and the piece of paper was gone.

It dawned on her that the woman had intentionally followed her to take the paper. Her curiosity now piqued, she rushed out to the street just in time to see a red hat turning the corner. *Good thing I didn't wear my high heels today*, she thought, and quickly followed a safe distance behind.

Three blocks later, the woman entered a nondescript apartment building with a child's bicycle propped against a bush in an overgrown front garden. Inside the doorway were labels identifying three tenants. The owner of the bicycle came out of the front door and smiled shyly at Veronica.

"Hello," she said. "I'm looking for the lady in a red hat who just came in here. Do you know where I can find her?"

The child pointed to the staircase and said, "Mrs. Andrews lives on the second floor, but she's visiting my mommy right now."

"She has something that belongs to me, and I would like it back. Could you ask her to come out and see me, please?"

About five minutes later, the woman came out.

"I believe you know why I'm here," she said, staring evenly at the woman. Without the hat that obscured most of her features, Veronica noticed that the woman was quite attractive. She appeared to be in her early forties with long, chestnut hair held with a clip at the nape of her neck. Her large brown eyes were red rimmed, and she clutched a handkerchief in her hand.

"Please come in to my friend's apartment," she sniffed, "and I'll explain my actions to you." The apartment was neat and tidy despite the rather shabby furnishings. The child's mother was sitting on a worn sofa and asked Veronica if she would like a cup of coffee.

"No, thank you, just an explanation," she said. With a heavy sigh, the woman sat down and began.

"My name is Diane Andrews. My ex-husband, Carl, was released from prison last month where he was doing time for armed robbery. He was part of the gang that robbed that mansion on Castle Hill a few years ago that was in the news. He swore he was through with that life and begged me to give him another chance, that he had enough money now so we could start again and finally live in style. He said he had the address of the house where the gang hid most of the valuables, and his share was waiting to be picked up.

"I needed to pay the rent and had just been laid off at my job," cried Diane, dabbing her eyes with the hanky. "Carol, here, loaned me some money, but I hate to owe people," she said, turning to her friend who squeezed her hand.

"I told Carl I wanted no part of stolen goods. I was about to pawn my engagement ring when you saw me at the shop. Carl had given me the paper with the address of the house, and I realized it had fallen out of my pocket. I saw you pick it up from the floor, and my heart leaped from my chest. I followed you, and, well, you know the rest."

Veronica sat quietly absorbing the story and the misery of the woman telling it. "Where is Carl now?"

"I don't know. He and another are the only ones left in the gang beside the boss, and Carl is scared. Believe me, the guy has never been scared of anyone or anything in his life, but Patch is dangerous and violent and wants everything for himself."

"Patch?"

"He lost an eye in prison trying to beat up another inmate. I guess the name just stuck."

Veronica thought a minute and asked, "Do you still have the paper?"

Diane fished around in her pocket and handed it to her. She stared at the address and said, "I think we should give this to the police and let them handle it."

"Carl will go back to prison. He was never an ideal husband, and he used to beat me when he had too much to drink, but he's all I have," she wailed. "Can't we just go there ourselves and see if they will listen to reason?"

"Something tells me this isn't such a good idea," said Veronica, "but you're so miserable, and I'm so curious. Do you know where this street is?"

There was something both pathetic and uplifting about Diane. She was obviously intelligent, and after hearing the story of her marriage to a man who was never going to be a model citizen, she decided she felt better with her rash decision to accompany Diane to a house in a shady neighborhood that contained stolen merchandise from a well publicized robbery of several years ago. *Maybe it is that curiosity bug Harry is always accusing me of*, she thought, *but if there is a way I can help this poor woman, I think I owe it to her to at least confront her husband and try to get her some money to pay her rent. Why should she be reduced to pawning her engagement ring?* The thought of that just went against her grain. She couldn't help but compare her situation to Diane's. Here she was, in a comfortable relationship with a good man of independent means who would do just about anything for her. She trusted him implicitly, and he had never given her any reason to doubt his commitment to her. She was a lucky woman to have such an upright man in her life.

She thought briefly about asking Harry to accompany them but decided not to say anything that would scare Diane, who needed to put to rest her ties with her husband. Maybe Veronica could convince her to leave him and forge a life of her own.

"How did you meet Carl?" she asked, her curiosity getting the better of her.

"I was going to night school to get a degree in library science and became friends with one of my classmates. We had coffee one day, and she asked me if I had a boyfriend. I told her I had just broken up with a man I had been seeing, and she suggested that I meet her brother for a blind date. It seemed like a good idea at the time, so I agreed. The first few dates went very well, and I was impressed with Carl and his dreams of wanting to get ahead in life. He was a

To Paint A Murder

mechanic and an electrician and liked to fix up cars and resell them. Although he only had a high school education, he said he had a good job with a friend who owned a garage. He took me to nice restaurants and was always a gentleman, and I found myself falling for him."

She sighed before going on. "I guess that's my problem; I believe everything people tell me. He said he liked that I wanted to better myself and after a few months of dating, he proposed. A justice of the peace married us, and for a short time, I was happy. I guess I was oblivious to the fact that he liked to gamble, and it didn't register with me that he had a problem with drink as well. Needless to say, his good job evaporated, and it was left to me to pay the bills. I had to leave school and take employment to keep a roof over our heads."

She sighed again and turned to Carol. "Thank goodness I have good friends and neighbors because I don't know what I would do otherwise."

Carol spoke up. "Carl used to hit her, and she would come downstairs and tell me her troubles. He would come and go at all hours, and I had to talk the landlord into letting them keep their apartment more than once."

Diane dabbed her eyes with her handkerchief. "I don't like to be a victim; that's not who I am, but there are some days that I just don't know what to do. That's why I want to see what this house contains and tell Carl that I will not stand for his nonsense any longer. I put my dreams on hold for him, and he has lied and cheated on me since the day we got married."

"He is going out with other women?" said Veronica. "After *all* you've done for him?"

"I found out he was seeing his ex-wife, a person that he didn't bother to tell me even existed. When I asked his sister about it, she admitted he had an ex-wife, but she assumed he had told me about her. What we didn't know was that they were still in touch, and he was wining and dining her while I was trying to come up with the rent money. When I confronted him with it, he swore he would give her up, that he had good prospects in a new job, and that he loved me more than ever for standing by him."

After hearing her story, Veronica resolved to help Diane in any way she could. They made plans to go to the house the next evening.

CHAPTER 6

The two women set off just as the sun was setting. The address was in a part of town that Veronica would never have wandered to by herself. As they walked together silently, each with her own thoughts, a large, dilapidated-looking house came into view at the end of a quiet cul-de-sac. Even early spring buds on the few sparse trees couldn't dispel the gloom of the place. The facade was badly in need of paint, and the boarded-up windows and front door added to the sinister atmosphere.

Glancing around nervously, they pulled their coats around them for warmth and walked around to the side of the house looking for another entrance. They found a back door with a broken window that Veronica was able to pry open. They entered noiselessly and with caution and saw a single lightbulb with a frayed wire hanging from the ceiling. It still worked and shed light on a butler's pantry that was stacked from floor to ceiling with cardboard boxes. A flashlight was on the counter and guided them through to the dining room where they stopped short.

"Look at all this stuff," whispered Diane.

More open boxes filled the space. Sculpture and crystal

overflowed as the arc of light from the flashlight revealed a treasure trove. Rolled up oriental carpets were haphazardly thrown against the wall fighting for space with stacks of silver trays.

"It's like King Tut's tomb in here!" exclaimed Diane. "No wonder Carl didn't want to give this up. It's as quiet as a tomb too."

They wandered to the living room, also overflowing with cartons. The worn carpet did not quite mask the creaking floorboards.

"I wonder what's in this closet?" asked Diane, turning the doorknob. The door swung open easily, and the zippered plastic clothing bag hanging on the inside hook almost knocked her down. Veronica, curious as well, crept over with the flashlight. They gasped and clutched each other in terror. Hanging out of the clothing bag they saw the white face of a dead man, glassy eyes staring at nothing, a knife protruding from his chest.

"Oh my God, it's Carl," gasped Diane, her hand covering her mouth in terror.

A sudden noise from the floor above registered in their consciousness and they darted to the kitchen and out the back door. Not being familiar with the neighborhood made little difference. They kept running until they found themselves in front of an all-night drugstore. Once inside, out of the cold wind and with their hands wrapped around mugs of hot coffee, the women stared at each other without speaking as they tried to take in what they had just seen.

"I can't believe Carl is dead," cried Diane, finally breaking the silence. "I always knew he would come to a bad end if he kept up with that gang, but to be killed in that way..."

"We have to report this to the police now," whispered Veronica, glancing over her shoulder. "They'll have to reopen the original investigation."

"I can't get involved in this. Carl is my ex-husband, but I have no reason to kill him, and *I* would become the chief suspect in his murder."

"Isn't that a little far-fetched? I mean, it has nothing to do with you, Diane."

"That's a chance I'm not willing to take. Carl always thought the reason the police never caught up with Patch was that he was paying someone off in the department to look the other way. He always said protection money was part of doing business."

Another late-night customer came in to the drugstore and took a seat at the far end of the counter. His coat collar was turned up to his ears and a cap was pushed down over his eyebrows. He unfolded a newspaper, ordered a cup of coffee, and remained unnoticed by the other customers.

"What I can't understand is why Carl was killed, Diane. I mean, there's a big difference between robbery and murder. What's in that house worth murdering over?"

Diane let out a little sob and clutched her handbag close to her chest. "I'll never forgive him for putting me in this position—never! He must have been in the way, and someone was threatened enough to kill him in cold blood."

"Do you still have the paper with the address on it? Let me look at it again." Diane opened her bag, fished around, and handed it to her.

"That's odd. I never noticed these before." Veronica squinted, took out her harlequin glasses, and pointed to tiny marks on the upper right-hand side. "These look like a series of numbers, like a safe combination. We have to see if there's a safe in the house. I'll bet the reason for the murder is in that safe."

"Are you mad?" cried Diane. "I'm not nosy enough to take my life in my hands. Look what happened to Carl, and what if the person who made that noise we heard is still there?"

"It could have been a rodent or a cat or something else that made the noise. I've been in plenty of old houses; noises just come with the territory."

"And what about Carl? We just can't leave him there, can we?"

"He can't do us any harm; he's dead! Why don't we go back tomorrow and things will look better in the daylight."

The man with the newspaper got up from the counter, glanced over at the women, and walked out. At the same time, they both looked up to see a face...with an eyepatch disappear out the door.

"Oh my God, it's Patch," cried Diane. "He must have heard every word we said." She got up quickly from the counter. "That's it. I'm not waiting around to be carved up like Carl."

Veronica clutched at her sleeve and pushed her back down on the stool. "We have to think this out carefully.

Carl must have gone back to get whatever is in the safe, and Patch was waiting for him. I have to say this guy is a cool customer. A dead body is in the house, and he's in here drinking coffee."

It suddenly dawned on her that Patch knew they were there, had probably caused the noise they heard, and decided to follow them.

"We have to find out what's in that safe."

"Is it worth our lives?" asked Diane. "I mean, I'm more than a little bit curious too, but this is a dangerous game we're playing."

Veronica thought a moment. "I've got an idea. I have a boyfriend who is devoted to me. Harry owns a gun because he lives in Boston in an art-filled home and always tells me a handy weapon is easier to own than a hungry guard dog. I'll call and ask him to go with us to the house early tomorrow morning. He's always accusing me of being nosy, but I'll bet anything he will be nosy enough himself to come with us."

Diane sat quietly.

"Come on," urged Veronica. "Aren't you just a little bit curious about what's in that safe?"

"I don't know," she said finally. "Is it wise to involve someone else, even if he has a gun to protect us?"

"You don't know Harry like I do. Don't worry. I'll talk him into going along with our plan and give him several good reasons why this isn't such a harebrained idea."

Diane didn't notice that Veronica crossed her fingers behind her back.

CHAPTER 7

Early the next day, Veronica called Harry and told him her plan. He was surprisingly calm about his girlfriend of three years asking him to bring a gun to a house that she and a new acquaintance broke in to that held the proceeds from a well publicized robbery.

Veronica met Carol at her apartment. "Harry is being a dear about all this. To him, this is an adventure to brighten an otherwise dull day."

"It won't be a dull day if someone finds us snooping around a house full of stolen property and a dead body."

"You seem to have accepted Carl's demise a little better today. Are you missing him?"

"How can I miss a wife beater, jailbird, and a cheat? What I miss is the promise of Carl, the man who was sweet and gentle and kind when I met him. Greed turned him into another person, and my choice of husband worked against me. But I still feel we should go to the police."

"Harry agrees, but thinks we should wait until we find out what's in the safe."

All three set out during a driving rain, making visibility and resolve a challenge. When the morning mist cleared, the house was very much the same. Veronica parked her car behind some overgrown bushes and then they waited to see if the silent neighborhood held any surprises. They crept to the back door and were able to gain entry easily. Harry went in first and kept his hand firmly on his weapon. They kept their distance from the closet that contained Carl's body and slowly ascended the stairs, eyes and ears straining for any sounds.

At the top of the stairs, they split up, hugging the walls and creeping along slowly. It appeared they were alone in the house.

"Would the safe be in plain sight?" whispered Veronica, as they entered an empty room.

"There's your answer straight ahead," said Harry, pointing to a large, old-fashioned heavy safe with an elaborate dial. "What's the combination?" Diane produced the paper, and Harry twirled the lock. Nothing happened.

"Here, let me try," said Veronica, pushing her harlequin glasses back up her nose.

"I don't know why you wear those things," said Harry. "You see better without them."

"They're a fashion statement, Harry, but men don't seem to understand these things."

"Let's try to concentrate on opening this safe, shall we?" whined Diane. "I'm a wreck wondering if it's rigged to blow up in our faces!"

"You've been watching too many television cop shows," said Harry, as Veronica slowly continued to turn the dial.

"Wait," he exclaimed. "I just heard a click."

A smiling Veronica slowly opened the safe door.

"You little beauty. That's my girl," he said, hugging her.

They all leaned in to peer into a dark...empty cavity.

"Nothing!" cried Diane. "All that work for nothing!"

Three dejected people sat down on the floor to think.

"Looks like someone beat us to it, if indeed there was anything in here at all," said Harry.

"We are right back where we started," cried Diane, searching in her pocket for a hanky.

"Now we have to go to the police. I'll go back to the shop and call Joe Banks."

"How do you plan on explaining our little adventure today?" asked Harry, getting up again to peer into the empty safe.

"Just tell him the truth, I guess. I'll turn over the paper to him, and Joe will know what to do."

"If you don't mind," said Harry, "please leave my name out of this. My family would not be thrilled to hear I'm mixed up in a murder and robbery case. I have to think of their reputation as well as my own."

The next few weeks brought a flurry of recognition to Veronica's Vintage as customers heard about her involvement in a major robbery and murder. Joe Banks was protective of her and said it was his experience that people would soon forget and go on to the next big thing the newspapers wrote about. But Veronica didn't forget, and the idea of her now good friend Diane having to be questioned by the police regarding her ex-husband's death depressed her. She recognized that Diane was a good person, and she was determined to be supportive. She encouraged her to return to school and obtain her degree. She knew Diane had the intelligence and drive to make a new life for herself and, even in the face of all the publicity about Carl, she kept her chin up and knew she could have a better life.

To bring Veronica out of her funk, Harry invited her to his Beacon Hill house for dinner one night. The chef prepared a delicious meal, and the table was set with candles, beautiful old family silver, and crisp linen. She carried her wineglass to the living room and admired the furnishings.

"Your paintings are beautiful, Harry. I never get tired of looking at them. Is this one new?" she asked, peering at a particularly nice landscape.

"A recent auction acquisition," he said. "Yes, my collection always brings me great pride and joy."

They sat down together on the chesterfield couch. "I still can't thank you enough for coming to my rescue. I don't know that I would have had the courage to go back to that house if you weren't there. I always feel safe with you."

"I daresay Carl got what he had coming to him. He probably tried to double-cross his partner, Patch, and held out on his share of the sale of the paintings."

"Well, I'll always be grateful you were there. Diane is too."

The next day Diane came in to the shop looking happier than Veronica had seen in weeks. The police had exonerated her of any involvement in the robbery, and she was able to get a part-time job at the library in between attending classes. With money now coming in, she paid back her neighbor and treated herself to a new hairdo and some clothes.

"You look wonderful, Diane. No more red hats?"

"No more red hats, Ronnie. I'm starting a new chapter in my life. No more robberies with missing paintings and empty safes for me."

"Speaking of that, Harry said something strange to me last night. He said Patch was holding out on his share of the paintings. Do you remember ever mentioning Patch's name to Harry, or the fact that paintings were involved?"

"I don't think so. No, I'm pretty sure I didn't. I thought only we knew about Patch, and as he seems to have disappeared, I've forgotten all about him."

The bell over the door tinkled, and Joe Banks walked in looking pensive.

"Hi, Joe. What, no latte and croissants this morning?" she said, eyeing his empty hands.

"This isn't a social call, Ronnie, and I'm glad you're here too, Diane. A man's body with no ID was found floating facedown near the docks early this morning. When they hauled him out of the water, he was wearing an eyepatch and a knife in his chest."

"Oh my God!" they cried in unison.

"This robbery is now a double murder investigation. A special crime task force from Boston has been assigned to the case. Some of the paintings have been recovered from a well-known fence in New Hampshire, and because it is across state lines, the FBI is now involved."

"I wonder what Patch's role was in all this?" asked Veronica.

"My department has had an eye on him for some time. It turns out Carl and Patch were cell mates, and we think they were both recruited for this heist from prison. Whoever is behind this has some pretty powerful connections. There's no room for amateur sleuthing here, ladies. I want your word that you'll leave the detecting to the professionals."

They looked at each other and nodded in the affirmative.

"Now that all the gang members that we know of from the original Castle Hill robbery are dead, there has to be someone still alive who pulled the strings. That's the guy we want...the puppeteer. He's ruthless, extremely dangerous, and knows his way around the art world."

"What about the rest of the stuff we saw in boxes at the house?" asked Veronica.

"All that is window dressing, the leavings. We now know that it was the paintings they were after, worth millions."

Diane asked, "And the safe and combination to the safe that was on the paper?"

"There is a tie-in, but we don't know what it is yet. My guess is that the safe contained incriminating evidence that identifies the mastermind behind the robbery. Somehow, he got to the safe before you did. Once we know who took that evidence, we'll know who stole the paintings and killed those two men."

CHAPTER 8

Business at Veronica's Vintage continued to be brisk for the next few weeks, and she had several requests from customers to visit their homes for appraisals and possible buying opportunities. One woman had beautiful oil paintings, and Veronica asked her if they were for sale. As they were family heirlooms to be passed down to her children, she declined.

"They are all beautiful, and I can understand why you would never want to part with them."

"Thank you," said the woman. "I had them appraised last year at the Artemis Gallery downtown and was very happy to hear their current value. Mr. Gordon was most helpful. If you ever need their services, I highly recommend them."

Veronica went back to the store with her purchases and thought about what the woman had said. She had two or three paintings that were part of Aunt Gillian's legacy to her and decided to call in at the gallery and get them appraised. She had taken photos of all the items she inherited for insurance purposes, and when she got back to her apartment that night, she looked them up. She thought of asking Harry's opinion of the gallery and Mr. Gordon, but the idea flew out of her head.

The next day before she opened the shop, she stopped in at the Artemis Gallery which was housed in a classic building with a marble facade with twin Doric columns and a discreet brass sign over the door.

"Good morning, I'm Giles Gordon. May I help you?" asked a dapper-looking gentleman in a charcoal-gray, three-piece suit, a pale-pink striped shirt, and a gray silk tie with hunting motifs. A gold pocket watch chain with a carved stone intaglio fob dangled from his vest, and his well cut gray hair and neat mustache gave him a benign and professional look.

"Hello," said Veronica. "I own the vintage shop a few streets over, and one of my customers highly recommended you as an art appraiser."

"And who might that be?" he smiled, showing a row of perfect teeth.

"Mrs. Endicott and she said you were most helpful in valuing her paintings."

"Ah, a lovely lady from a fine, old, local family. It can be said her antecedents actually did come over on the *Mayflower* and eventually became one of the founding families of Bromfield. They grew wealthy in the China Trade; sea captains whose ships were laden with porcelain, whale oil, and ivory."

"How well informed you are, Mr. Gordon."

"I'm a bit of a local historian. How can I be of service?"

Veronica took out the photos of her paintings and asked

him what his appraisal fee would be. He took them over to an ornately carved partner's desk, picked up a magnifying glass with a staghorn handle, and examined the photos. He asked if she was interested in selling.

"Not really; not yet, at any rate. They are part of my inheritance from my dear late aunt, and it occurred to me that I really need to insure them."

The telephone rang in another room. Mr. Gordon excused himself and hurried to answer it. As she walked around the gallery trying not to listen in on the conversation, it was obvious that angry words were being exchanged. Eventually, Mr. Gordon came back to the desk.

"I'm sorry about that, but I must go to my workroom and retrieve something for a customer who is coming by in a few minutes. Would you like to stay, and we can resume our chat? I really would like to talk to you about these photos."

She looked at her watch. "I have about a half hour to spare."

"Excellent. I'll just go to the back room before my customer comes in. Make yourself at home. We really have some wonderful pictures on display. I'll be a few minutes."

He disappeared, and she resumed looking at the array of artists' pictures the gallery represented. The prices of some of the works made her eyes water, and she wondered, not for the first time, that the other half lived very well indeed.

She found herself back at the desk and, as she reached for the photos, her eye caught a familiar name on a calling card. She glanced around to see if she was being observed, picked up the card, and read, "Harry Hunt, Principal, Artemis Gallery."

Harry never mentioned he owned a gallery, she thought. *I mean, he might as well own one with all the artwork in his house*, and she wondered again why he never told her.

The front door opened, and a man looking decidedly out of place in the establishment he was standing in came forward. He was wearing faded denim jeans with frayed hems, a stained work shirt, dirty boots, and had sandy hair badly in need of a wash. They stood for a minute eyeing each other when Mr. Gordon came out from the back room holding an envelope.

"It's all there," he said, handing it to the man.

"Should I count it?"

"Please, don't insult my intelligence," snarled Mr. Gordon.

Without saying another word, the man turned on his heels and stormed out.

"Sorry about that. As they say, you just can't get good help these days. He's a carpenter who did some work for me and came highly recommended. I still think I was overcharged."

"I know what you mean," said Veronica, looking him squarely in the eye. "To keep costs down, my boyfriend, Harry Hunt, helped me open my vintage shop."

The silence was deafening, but there was no change of expression or indication that he had ever heard of Harry.

"Oh, look at the time," she said, glancing at her watch.

"I'll have to come back later to make an appointment. I'd like to follow up on our conversation."

"With pleasure," he said, escorting her to the door.

She didn't notice him watching her from the window. When she was out of sight, he picked up the phone on his desk to make a hurried call.

Later that afternoon, Harry dropped by the shop. Looking up from the window display she was working on, Veronica smiled and asked, "To what do I owe this surprise visit? Isn't this neighborhood just a bit far from your usual haunts in the city?" This was going to be an interesting conversation, she thought.

"Just want to see how my girl is doing and maybe try to interest you in a lobster dinner."

"Oh, you sweet talker. I'm always interested in a lobster dinner, but first I'd like to stop in at the local art gallery and make an appointment for an appraisal. Do you mind? It won't take a minute."

Veronica locked the store, and they strolled over to Artemis. Giles Gordon was at his desk doing some paperwork as they walked in, and he looked up.

"Hello again. I never did get your name this morning."

"Veronica Howard and this is my friend, Harry Hunt," she said smoothly.

"How do you do?" Harry said, proffering his hand.

"A pleasure to meet you," said Mr. Gordon. "Are you an art lover too? You look familiar somehow."

"I dabble now and then. Maybe you've seen me at the

auction houses in town."

"That must be it. Miss Howard came in this morning with photos of some paintings and wanted to inquire about me possibly appraising them."

The next few minutes were passed in polite conversation, and neither man showed any signs of recognition. She took it all in, and, after making an appointment for later in the week, they left the gallery.

Even though she was eating her favorite dinner, Veronica couldn't focus on the food. She kept glancing at Harry wondering why he chose to take part in the elaborate charade she had just witnessed. She had a sinking feeling about it and needed to connect the dots. She had to discuss it with someone who would understand. With a rueful smile, Veronica realized that her old friend, Mandy, wouldn't understand. She couldn't go to Joe Banks either just yet, so that left Diane. She would talk to Diane tomorrow.

CHAPTER 9

As it happened, Diane stopped by Veronica's Vintage the next day carrying a takeout bag from the bakery down the street.

"Don't tell me you're on a diet because I bought croissants and some of those lovely sugar cookies," she said opening the bag.

"Yummy. Pull up a chair, Diane; we have to talk." After they had settled down, she recounted her trip to Artemis.

"Are you sure you read the card correctly? Why would Harry pretend he had no interest in the gallery or ever having met that man before? What's he hiding from you?"

"It was Harry's name I read, make no mistake. I thought I knew him very well, and I'm almost positive it was him that I saw at the hotel reception that one night."

The cream and gold old-fashioned French phone rang on her desk.

"Oh, hi Harry, I was just thinking of you," she said, waving at the phone with her other hand to get Diane's attention. She listened without speaking for some minutes.

"I'm sure Diane still has it. I'll ask her to give it to me. What are you going to do with it?" She listened some more.

"All right, see you at six." She put the receiver back and stared at Diane. "Harry wants to meet me tonight for dinner and to see the paper with the combination on it. Says he has an idea what it's all about."

Diane fished in her bag and took out the crumpled paper, smoothing it out on her knee.

"I made a copy at the library, but something told me to hold on to the original."

"Let me see it again," said Veronica, reaching for the paper. She held it up to her desk lamp and then held it up to a ten-power jeweler's loupe.

"What are you looking for," giggled Diane, "a message written in invisible ink like an old-time movie plot?"

Veronica put the paper down on her lap. She wasn't laughing.

"Either my eyesight is fading, or my imagination is running away from me, but here, take a look at the extreme bottom left corner. What do you see?"

Diane grabbed the paper out of her hand and held it up to the loupe and leaned into the light.

"Well, well, what do you know? It looks like there's tiny writing, almost like hen scratching. Why didn't we notice this before? We were so busy looking at the safe numbers, we entirely missed this." She looked again. "Wait a minute; it looks like Arabic to me."

"Do we know anyone who speaks Arabic?"

"Yes, as a matter of fact, I do. My boss at the library has a degree in Middle Eastern art and languages. She could read this." She looked at her watch and reached for the phone. "We're in luck," she said excitedly. "Mrs. Chambers is at her desk now for a short time. She'll take a look at the paper for us."

"Well, then, let's go," said Veronica, grabbing her coat and turning the open sign on the door to closed on their way out.

The Bromfield Public Library was housed in a typical postwar New England building painted white with gray shutters and trim. It was situated across from the Town Hall, and next to the post office, so parking was always at a premium. Diane was able to find a spot at the rear of the building for employees only, and they entered from a side door. Mrs. Chambers, the head librarian, had her office next to the elevator and looked up and smiled when they entered. Diane introduced Veronica and explained what they were asking for. She took the paper and held it up to a fourteen-power loupe and proceeded to decipher the writing by talking to herself, then translating to English on the pad of paper in front of her.

"How very interesting," she said. "Yes, *very* interesting."

Both women were holding their breath waiting for her to continue.

"It seems to be a description of two signed nineteenth-century oil paintings; one a Dutch nautical scene and the other a landscape by a fairly famous painter. Does that information ring any bells with you?" she asked.

Diane spoke up and said not really, but they did wonder

why it was written in Arabic. Mrs. Chambers held up the paper again. "No, that's all it says, just the description. Here, I'll write down the translation and give it to you."

They thanked her profusely, and Diane made a copy of both papers, handing one to Veronica. She said she wanted to look up something in the reference library that would only take a minute. While waiting, Veronica wandered over to the magazine section and absentmindedly picked up a copy of *Antiques Digest*. Her eye immediately went to an article alerting the public to an art heist that the FBI was investigating and asking the public for any information to help them. It described the two paintings they were inquiring about. She jumped up and made a copy of the article and handed it to Diane when she came back. She was determined not to tell Harry about their findings until she heard what he had to say at dinner tonight.

"I can't believe this coincidence, Diane." They both squealed and then heard the man at the table next to them say "shhh." They left immediately and decided in the car to tell Joe Banks about their findings when Veronica returned to the shop. She called the police station and was told that Officer Banks was out on patrol and left a message for him to call her immediately. An hour later, he walked into the shop.

"A sight for sore eyes," she cried. "If you have some time, I have a story to tell you." She recounted their findings at the library, but she didn't include that Harry wanted to see the paper.

Joe frowned and said, "This paper is evidence in a

robbery and murder investigation, Ronnie. You should have mentioned it sooner."

"We only just saw the writing and had it translated, Joe. I called you immediately when I returned to the store."

"Did you ever think about the possibility that the people involved might know you have this and go after you to get it back? We are talking about people here who kill to get what they want. You're playing Russian roulette with your life," he said, slamming his fist on the desk for emphasis.

"If you're trying to scare me, Joe, you're doing a great job!"

"I'm trying to get through to you that you cannot run around and play amateur detective. Your life is worth more than your curiosity, isn't it?"

She knew he was right, but it was too late to back down now. She had to see that Diane was taken care of and that her questions concerning the paintings were answered.

"Give the paper to me now, and I'll enter it in as evidence."

She handed it over to Joe, and he said he would give her a receipt for it later.

CHAPTER 10

She had mixed feelings when six o'clock finally came and had a hard time finding the restaurant Harry suggested, which turned out to be a small, out-of-the-way roadhouse about five miles from Bromfield Center. It surprised her that he would want to eat here as he was a gourmet who employed a private chef and was fussy about food and dining. The place looked seedy and was located on a road that wasn't used much since a new major highway was built nearly ten years before. The low building sat on a concrete block foundation, and the siding, painted a faded red with brown trim, looked as though it needed work. The restaurant was set back from the road, and the small rear parking area, which contained three or four cars, was dimly lit.

Harry was waiting in his Porsche when she drove in. He was smiling when he jumped out, kissed her cheek, and escorted her to the door. When they were seated, she looked around at the few diners and wondered again why he had chosen this particular place. He seemed to read her mind and explained he had heard the food was exceptional, an undiscovered gem of a place, and wanted to surprise her.

The menu and food turned out to be mediocre at best. Veronica sat quietly while wondering when he would bring up the subject of the paper. She was halfway through her salad when he casually asked if she had it with her. She reached in her pocketbook and silently handed the copy to him without the Arabic writing. He took it, held it up to the light, looked at her, then handed it back without speaking.

The atmosphere was stilted and awkward after that, and neither of them attempted to discuss the situation. It was clear they were unsatisfied with how the evening was moving along, and both seemed determined not to break the ice and confront the other.

Veronica felt sad and somehow used and couldn't understand why Harry was treating her like a stranger. He was always so upbeat, and their ability to laugh was part of the glue that kept them together. Tonight, he was a stranger to her, and it was a side of him that she neither wanted to know or like. He was obviously keeping things from her, and, if the truth be told, she was doing the same to him.

Neither was interested in lingering over coffee and dessert, so they both walked silently to the parking lot. He awkwardly opened the door to her car, and she could hold her tongue no longer.

She turned to him and cried, "What's going on, Harry? What are you hiding from me?" He raised his arm, and her consciousness registered an explosion of stars and pain as she crumpled to the ground.

She didn't know how long she lay on the cold pavement;

she only knew it hurt her head to move. It took a few minutes to register where she was. When she finally glanced at her watch, she saw it was 12:30 a.m. Harry was nowhere in sight. She forced herself slowly to her feet and took great gulps of air to try to clear her head. She saw her keys were in the ignition and decided to drive back to the shop instead of going to her apartment, a trip she would probably not be able to make in her present condition. She looked around the deserted parking lot trying to piece together how she got there and trying not to cry out of frustration and pain. She sat in her car and decided crying was a good option and reached for the box of tissues she kept on the dashboard.

Posy Place was deserted at that hour of the morning, and as she put the key in the shop front door, the only lights that could be seen through the fog that had descended were the old-fashioned lamps on the sidewalk outside her store. Her head still hurt. She managed to find the bottle of aspirin she kept in her desk drawer. It was more comfortable to stay in the dark, so she carefully picked her way through the store to the big, dark blue velvet sofa she had hoped to sell but now was very glad she didn't.

The realization that she did not know her boyfriend of three years hurt as much as the bump on her head, and she started to cry again. *How could he do this to me?* she thought. *What are you hiding, and why can't you confide in me and trust that I will stand by you, no matter what?* She always thought Harry was on her side and always felt safe with him. But after tonight, she was confused and mad.

Damn it and damn you, Harry Hunt, she thought. She tried to get up but immediately felt nauseated. She lowered her head slowly and started to piece together the night's happenings. Now she realized that when he examined the paper, he immediately knew the Arabic writing was not present. Was that why he hit me? she wondered in frustration, and was he somehow connected to the robberies? Why would he insist on meeting me at an out-of-the-way and, frankly, inferior, restaurant in the first place? Harry was a gourmet. He employed his own chef, for pity's sake, and that place would never, *ever* measure up to his high culinary standards. Was it because he was not known there...or hiding from someone?

Her head was a kaleidoscope of questions going around in circles with no answers. It always came back to the lack of trust she felt at this particular moment. The Harry she cared about would never have left her in the early hours of the morning, cold, alone, and injured.

She decided to call the police station and report the assault. When the squad car pulled up, blue lights flashing, she decided to leave out Harry's name. She reported to the two officers that she was involved in a mugging by an unknown person in the restaurant parking lot after her dinner partner had left in his car. She could not describe her attacker, nor was she able to give them a vehicle color, model number, or license plate number.

When the police asked if anything was missing, she replied no. She now knew a copy of the paper wasn't what

Harry wanted; it was the Arabic writing he was after. When she didn't give it to him, he lashed out and hit her hard on the head and left her there, alone, in the dark. That was the reality, and she was devastated. After they left, she put her head back down and slept a deep and dreamless sleep.

The morning sun was streaming through the front window when she finally awoke. The fog of last night in the atmosphere and in her head was gone. She splashed water on her face and combed her hair before calling the station house again. A new day was dawning at Veronica's Vintage and with Veronica Howard.

Officer Joe Banks walked in a half hour later with coffee and freshly baked lemon Danish.

"Fresh out of the oven," he said, putting the box on her desk. "Are you okay, because you look like hell! Can I drive you to the hospital to get you checked out?"

"I'm all right. I told the officers I made the report to that I don't need medical attention."

"When I heard the news at the station this morning, I had a feeling you were involved even before I read your name. I'm going to be straight with you, Ronnie. I don't think you reported the whole story. What are you leaving out?"

She thought a moment, then told Joe that Diane's late husband, Carl, and his equally late partner in crime, Patch, had admitted to paying protection money to someone in the Bromfield Police Department.

"I didn't want to report that kind of allegation, Joe, especially coming from two career criminals. Do you think there's any truth to it?"

She didn't have the heart to tell him she knew who wanted the paper and that she knew who her assailant was.

Veronica believed in God. She was brought up by two religious parents who insisted the family worship together regularly. When she became orphaned and Aunt Gillian took over her education, weekly attendance at Sunday school was part of her upbringing. Gillian was a volunteer at the local soup kitchen, and she took Veronica with her to help serve meals to the homeless and wash dishes. She believed in community service and looked in on her elderly neighbors, especially during the holidays, to make sure they were not alone. She instilled in her niece that God was as much a part of her life as breathing.

The fact that Harry felt as she did about religion now conflicted her more than ever. He and his family shared the same values as she, and that was one of the reasons they got along so well together. Now that he was acting so completely out of character, so against the solid and comfortable value system they had always shared made her angry and confused. How could someone you thought you knew so well do a complete turnaround and act in such an uncaring and hurtful way? She had no answers but vowed to find them.

Veronica asked God to help her. She prayed for His assistance and wrestled with her conscience about her feelings of betrayal at Harry's hands. There had to be a reasonable explanation for his behavior. She racked her brain for answers.

Maybe she did or said something to hurt his feelings. She knew she could be sarcastic sometimes. Did she make a cutting remark in jest that he couldn't forget or forgive?

She then realized she cared about him more than she wanted to admit. Harry was her friend and lover, and it was Harry who received Aunt Gillian's all-important stamp of approval. Gillian was an excellent judge of character, and she told her more than once that he was a person of quality.

"Look at the man," she would say. "The circumstance of his birth is just window dressing. Fall in love for the right reasons and don't be dazzled by all the rest."

But could she ignore what had happened? The man she thought she knew struck her, and the story that supported his action was silly and shallow. She was confused and conflicted once again.

CHAPTER 11

The day turned out to be bright and sunny, but she wasn't really aware of it. Her dark mood reflected the fitful sleep of the night before and all the questions she still had. She lived in Boston but worked exclusively in Bromfield and felt out of touch with the gossip she got on a regular basis working in the advertising business. She decided to call Mandy and ask if she could shed any light on the mystery of Harry's recent bizarre behavior without giving too much away.

Mandy answered on the second ring. "Nice to finally hear from the retail maven. How does it feel to be running your own show?"

"It's everything I hoped it would be, but I would appreciate a little help from my friends. When are you going to drop by for some serious retail therapy? I'm not that far from Boston, you know!"

"I know I haven't been in touch as much as I should, but lately, I don't know whether I'm coming or going with this new account. Frankly, I miss you like hell. Health food lunches, or *any* lunches, just aren't the same without my friend who listens to all my complaints."

"Actually, Mandy, I'm calling to ask a favor. Have you by any chance heard any rumors about Harry's family business? I mean, are they still solvent?"

"What a funny thing to ask. As far as I know, they are still rolling in money, and the account is rock solid. What's the matter? Have you two had a lover's quarrel?"

Leave it to my friend to get right to the heart of the matter. But I'm sure I'm doing the right thing by asking her. "No," she said cautiously, "it's not that. I heard somewhere that Harry might have made some bad investments, and, well, I just wanted to know if there was any truth to it."

"The Boston rumor mill is still grinding, but, no, I haven't heard anything negative about Harry or his family. You know if I did, I'd be on the phone to you faster than a new Prada bag offering. But if you're worried, why don't you ask him, Ronnie. I know he would tell you the truth."

She thought a moment, then plowed ahead. "Well, for your ears only, but I'm cooling a bit. After three years with Harry, things are getting stale between us, and I'm seriously thinking of moving on."

The silence was deafening. Finally, Mandy answered. "You really know how to drop a bombshell, don't you? Well, if you're serious, I have just the man for you. He's rich, he's handsome, he's single, he's—"

"Hang on, Mandy. If this guy is so great, why haven't *you* grabbed him?"

"I can't because he's my client. And you know if Old Man Styles ever got wind of an office romance, I would be out of a job, and I love my job."

"Fair enough. What does he do?"

"He owns his own successful business, a high-tech, state-of-the-art home security company with A-Listers and celebrities for clients. How about I fix you up on a blind date; get you out of your current doldrums?"

Brightening up, Veronica answered immediately. "You know, that's a great idea. I need a change, and he sounds perfect."

Mandy laughed again. "Just promise you'll give me a complete report. I'll see if he's free tomorrow night and have him call you."

Veronica knew from experience that Mandy's taste in men was eclectic at best. In fact, sometimes she thought her friend had serious lapses in judgment. Mandy's last heartthrob was a drummer in a rock band whose idea of dressing for dinner included torn jeans at the knees, a black tee shirt with the legend "Zonked Out" written on the front, dirty sneakers with Day-Glo orange soles, and a leather jacket covered with nail studs. He had a large tattoo of an American eagle on his neck that extended to who knew where.

Thankfully, her flavor of the month changed often. She didn't have to explain that now that she was an account executive for a larger and more important advertising agency, she had a certain social level to maintain. So when she suggested a new man, a client especially, she didn't know what her friend would say.

But Veronica was open to change now. Her heart was broken, and Mandy could sense the hurt in her voice. She could feel her friend was disappointed and disillusioned without knowing the details. Ronnie would tell her the whole story when she was ready. In the meantime, it couldn't hurt to introduce her to Tom, a man she would definitely keep for herself if she could. As she explained, office policy on dating clients seemed to be an industry thing, a policy that was in place with Acme and now at Styles & Company. So what? she thought. Handsome and nice, rich guys didn't grow on trees, and she was always ready for another challenge down the line.

Her tactful call to Tom Graham was met with great interest. It seemed he was available to meet a great new woman and his divorce and burgeoning new business venture had left him with little time to date.

Back at the shop, the phone rang.

"Veronica's Vintage. May I help you?"

A deep baritone voice asked to speak to Veronica Howard.

"Speaking," she answered, hoping the sexy voice at the other end was Mandy's client and not the usual salesman.

"Hi, I'm Tom Graham. Amanda Spencer gave me your phone number."

"Oh, hello, Tom. Yes, Mandy mentioned her newest and best ever client might call."

"Ah, the soft sell, I see," he said, laughing. "I can tell you used to be in advertising as well. But I understand you got out and now run your own business, just as I do. We definitely have some things in common."

He sounds great, she thought. *Maybe Mandy has hit the nail on the head this time.* They chatted for a while, and Tom asked her if she would like to join him for a drink that evening. They agreed to meet at the cocktail bar of the Copley Place Hotel in Boston at 7:00 p.m.

She hung up the phone and glanced in the mirror. *I desperately need a haircut*, she thought and called the salon down the street for an appointment. While there, she booked a manicure, pedicure, and facial as well. *Might as well go for broke*, she thought. She decided not to wear a vintage dress but rather, close the shop early and hit the department stores on the way home. It occurred to her that it had been a long time since she had looked forward to a night out with a new man. *I wonder what he looks like*, she mused, watching the stylist blow-dry her hair. *Mandy said he's handsome, and if he looks half as good as he sounds, then I'll be doing all right.*

The crimson sheath dress she bought matched her favorite pair of Jimmy Choo shoes, purchased in a mad moment when she had gotten her last raise at Acme. A liberal spray of her favorite scent, Chanel No. 5, a quick pat of her freshly styled hair, and she was out the door.

When she arrived at the hotel, the bar was noisy and packed with the after-work crowd enjoying the end of a busy day with their favorite tipple. She glanced at her watch. *Now, where is he?* she wondered, looking around the room.

"You must be the lovely Veronica," whispered a deep voice behind her.

"And what if I wasn't?" she asked, turning around to face a very tall and handsome man who more than slightly resembled Harrison Ford.

Be still my heart, she thought, and he answered, "I would apologize, then ask if I could buy you a drink." His smile was dazzling.

"Hello, Tom, we are both on time, I see," and she put out her hand for him to shake. Instead, he kissed and held it gently for a brief moment, gazing into her eyes. He guided her to a quiet table where they ordered martinis. "Something else we have in common," he said, trying not to be too obvious as he looked her over.

They glanced at the menu, both ordered clam chowder, broiled salmon, and a garden salad, then got down to quizzing each other about their marital status. Tom admitted to being recently divorced, citing his growing business as the cause. He never devoted enough time to his wife and young daughter, he admitted, regrets that he, no doubt, still harbored. He was quite surprised that Veronica had never married and wondered what fates had brought her here tonight.

"I don't have to tell you how much time is devoted to starting a business," he said, enjoying the chowder. "Always a million things to attend to and never enough hours in the day to get them done. People told me that I would have to invest in a start-up, but I was thinking in terms of money, not hours."

"I couldn't agree more," she said. "In my case, it isn't a nine-to-five situation. Often, I work after closing the store and on Sundays, as well. But, like you, I love what I do, so it's worth it. Who was it that said, 'When you enjoy your job, you're not really working'?"

"Is there a man in your life currently? Mandy hinted that you might have a boyfriend."

"There is, or rather, there *was*," she said. "Things have not been going well lately, and I just haven't had time to break it off. But I will, soon, I promise you that," she said with a hint of defiance in her voice.

He ordered another round of martinis, and they continued to discuss the pitfalls of business. She learned he had a workforce of eighteen people and his growing client list currently included several art galleries as well as private homes and business venues.

"My soon-to-be ex-boyfriend has a collection of fine art. Perhaps you installed security at his house."

"What's his name?" he asked.

"Harry Hunt and he lives on Beacon Hill."

Tom, almost choking on his drink, set the glass down on the table and stared. "What a coincidence," he said finally. "I have an appointment with him later this week to give him a quotation."

"Well, well. What a small world," said Veronica frostily. "You had better not mention my name, then."

He leaned over and took her hand in his. "Only if you promise that we can have dinner again this weekend," he whispered.

"I would be delighted." And she was. *I must remember to send Mandy a bouquet of flowers to thank her*, she thought.

CHAPTER 12

It was time to confront Harry about the attack. She had to find out why he hit her so brutally and left her in the early-morning hours, cold and alone. He never called her or offered any explanation, and she had to have answers. It saddened her that a person she had known and trusted for several years treated her with such disrespect. She was beginning to wonder if Harry was ill. If that were the case, then why haven't I seen the signs? How can a person be bright and sunny one minute, then violent and vengeful the next? It's almost as if he has an evil twin inside that takes over and strikes out at a moment's notice.

The phone rang. She answered on the second ring.

"Veronica," he started, "I want to meet you and give you an explanation."

The silence was deafening.

"Did you hear me, Veronica?"

"I have no interest whatsoever in meeting you anywhere that doesn't have at least one hundred people around," she sneered.

He sighed heavily. "I guess I deserve that, but you don't know the whole story."

"I've been waiting to hear the whole story for the last three days. You can tell me now, over the telephone, while keeping your distance."

"Okay. You've got to know that I had to leave you there alone that night because someone was pointing a gun at you!"

"Do you *really* expect me to believe that?" she cried. "I thought you cared for me, Harry. You've said so often enough."

"I do care, and I very much regret how things turned out, but I can't explain this over the phone. Please meet me—anywhere you like—so you can hear my side of the story."

She thought a moment and told him to meet her at the food court in the mall in Peabody, a city not far from Bromfield, in an hour's time. Harry was waiting for her when she arrived. They sat at a quiet table in full view of the busy department store entrance across the way. He looked as if he hadn't slept for several days, and the circles under his eyes were blue.

She folded her arms across her chest, scowled, and said, "Okay, the ball's in your court, Harry. I'm listening."

He took a deep breath and began. "Before we met for dinner that night, I received a phone call from a man who has been after me to invest in his business. He said he had heard from several sources that I had made some questionable investments in artwork that was forged, and unless I put money in his business as a silent partner, he would spread it around that I was a phony. I totally denied his allegations and challenged him to prove them. He argued that if I didn't help fund his operation, he would expose me.

"I told him I was on my way to take you to dinner, and he suggested that particular restaurant. He said if I didn't meet him there, he would go to the newspapers with the story that I was a fraud. I agreed to meet him later; then he surprised me by jumping out of the bushes, aiming a gun at you. I thought quickly and figured if I knocked you down and pushed you out of the way, he wouldn't be able to shoot you."

She thought a moment and said, "Well, you certainly did a good job. My head still hurts."

"I'm so sorry, Veronica, but I'm sure I saved your life."

"What's this guy's name, and what does he look like?"

"He has only ever identified himself as Smith. I know it sounds cheesy, but it's the truth. As to what he looks like, I haven't a clue. He was wearing a black mask, you know, like the Lone Ranger or Bat Boy."

Veronica didn't know whether to laugh or cry. Actually, she couldn't do either because it would probably hurt.

He saw the expression on her face. "Look, you've got to believe me. I wouldn't make this up. You know I would never do anything to hurt you; yet, I've managed to do just that."

He reached over to hug her, and she automatically leaned in to him. The story was too preposterous to be a lie, she thought, and really, would Harry ever deliberately hurt her?

At that moment he looked like a sad little boy who had

lost his favorite teddy bear. "I have to tell you that I reported the assault to the police, but I didn't say it was you."

"Oh, my dearest girl," he cried, holding her tightly. "You have to believe I only acted to save your life. You mean too much to me to ever lose you."

She had no doubt now that Harry was serious, but in her mind, she had already moved on. Tom was looking more like a white knight than Harry did.

"I have to think over what you've just told me. I'm so confused right now, and I think we should take a vacation from each other."

"I understand, Veronica, but please don't do anything rash. But you're right. What we need is time and space to think."

CHAPTER 13

Veronica went back to the store, her head spinning with the story Harry had just told her. She thought she knew him well, and her instincts suggested that perhaps he was an innocent victim of a con man. *Did he really act quickly to protect me, or was I just in the wrong place at the wrong time, and he was using me to protect his own skin?*

She had so many questions that had not been answered. Who is this mysterious Smith, and why did Harry want to see the paper with the Arabic writing. He obviously knew the paper I showed him is not the original. Is that paper what the con man was really after? It still bothered her that Harry took so long to contact her.

She wandered over to Aunt Gillian's picture and gazed at it. *Talk to me,* she thought. Tell me what to do. I need your advice now more than ever. She closed her eyes and mentally telegraphed her questions. I have the possibility of a new man in my life, but somehow I just can't let Harry go. He has betrayed my trust and hasn't given me a plausible explanation. Am I to believe his story about someone in a silly mask pointing a gun at me? Why would they, and is there a sinister reason why he is not telling me the whole truth?

She opened her eyes and tears ran down her cheeks as she tried to clear her mind. Thoughts began to assemble in the form of questions: Harry out of character; Harry covering up; Harry ill.

Then she thought of Tom and made comparisons. He is so forthcoming about his business and private life. He's built a company to be proud of from scratch, not one just handed to him. She knew from experience that it takes someone who has struggled to get what they want out of life to value it more. *We are more like kindred spirits, better suited. Oh, I'm so confused.*

Veronica spent the afternoon rearranging store displays. A new customer came in who wanted to buy jewelry. She was going to a party and didn't want to wear her expensive necklace but rather a nicely made faux piece that would fool the eye.

All of a sudden it hit her that maybe the idea of switching phony for real was behind the robbery. Why hadn't she thought of it before? Maybe the con man was blackmailing Harry to get the paper from her in exchange for keeping his mouth shut about exposing Harry's supposed dodgy art collection. It certainly fit in with what she knew.

The bell over the door announced another customer. Veronica looked up to see Tom coming into the shop holding a large bouquet of flowers.

"What a nice surprise," she said, taking the arrangement from him.

"I thought I would brighten your afternoon," he said, planting a light kiss on her lips.

"You've certainly done that," she said, placing the flowers in a glass vase.

He slowly turned around taking in the store contents and displays. "So this is Veronica's Vintage. I approve; yes, I do approve. I thought we might have that dinner tonight, if you have no other plans." It was almost closing time, so she turned off the lights and locked the door.

The summer evening was perfect, warm with a slight breeze blowing, and you could smell the ocean if you breathed in deeply. People were walking together slowly, and snippets of conversation were punctuated with laughter. No one seemed to be in much of a hurry, and the pace was relaxed and languid.

They walked to a small family-owned bistro that specialized in French country cooking and were seated at a table under a green-striped umbrella in a quiet courtyard. Birds were chirping, and the bushes that surrounded the space gave them privacy. Both ordered onion soup, coq au vin, and the pear tart. The wine was a cool and crisp Beaujolais. She casually asked if he had met with Harry during the week and noticed for the first time a slight tic in his left eye when he mentioned Harry's name.

"It's funny you should mention it. I wasn't able to get in touch with him, and he never returned my calls. I'll try him again next week."

They spent the evening talking about their work and

personal lives. She learned that Tom had once lived in the south of France working as a security consultant for an American company. He told several anecdotes about living in France that made her weak with laughter. *He certainly has led an exciting life,* she thought. *No wonder he's so sophisticated.* His easy demeanor and beautiful blue eyes made her forget all about the odd week she was having.

They walked back to the store to get her car. Tom suddenly took her in his arms, kissed her passionately, and suggested they drive back to her apartment and continue their night together. She wanted to do just that, but for some reason, she hesitated. He picked up on it and said he didn't want to force her to do anything quickly. She explained that since they had just met, perhaps they should get to know each other a bit more. His smile told her he agreed, and they drove back to Boston in their own cars.

Veronica called Mandy when she got home and recounted her evening. Mandy couldn't believe she didn't want to spend the night with Tom. She reminded her friend that he was handsome, charming, wealthy, and intelligent and asked what her problem was. Surely, it couldn't be that she still had feelings for Harry, especially now that she had met Tom.

But that was just it. In her heart of hearts, Veronica couldn't push Harry aside, even though she had gone through a horrible night of fright, the memory of which still lingered. She went to bed conflicted and confused.

The next day she decided to return to the Artemis

Gallery under the pretext of going forward with the insurance appraisal. Giles Gordon was sitting behind his desk talking on the phone and looked quite surprised when she walked in. He quickly hung up and asked if he could assist her. She said she had decided to go ahead with the appraisal, and he handed her some forms to fill out. She could feel his eyes on her as she wrote.

"I understand you acquire paintings at auctions on behalf of clients," she said, tapping the pencil on the desk.

"Yes, that is part of my service. Often when bidders realize a well-known collector is after a certain picture, they will bid the price up just for spite or jealousy. There's a lot of that in the art world, I can tell you. But when I bid, they don't know if it's for my gallery or a client."

"Have you ever bid on behalf of my boyfriend, Harry Hunt?"

"I'm not really at liberty to say, Miss Howard. Why don't you ask Harry?"

"Oh, so you do know him, then?"

"Mr. Hunt is well known in the art world; I've met him a number of times."

That's interesting, she thought. Why did he pretend not to know Harry when they met here last week? She felt Gordon staring at her again and handed him the completed forms.

A brainstorm suddenly hit her, and she asked, "Another friend, Tom Graham, has suggested I install a burglar alarm in my shop. Would you recommend his company to do the job?"

At the mention of Graham's name, Gordon fairly leaped out of his chair, narrowly missing spilling a cup of coffee on his desk.

"My, you do know some heavy hitters, don't you?" he commented, trying to regain his composure. Suddenly, his desk phone rang.

If you ask me, thought Veronica, *you were just saved by the bell.*

He cupped his hand over the receiver. "I'll be awhile on this call, I'm afraid. Why don't I get back to you in a day or two, and we'll make an inspection appointment."

She stood and thanked him and hurried out the door. His reflection in the window told her he was following her progress down the street.

CHAPTER 14

Later that day, Diane stopped by the shop looking very chic in a navy tailored suit and matching designer handbag. Veronica complimented her on her new look and Diane told her the library was so happy with her work that they were sending her to an out-of-town conference for a few days. Her happiness was so evident, and Veronica was pleased by the turnaround her new friend's life was taking.

"I can't remember when I've been so at peace," said Diane. "I've even been on a date with a lovely man who has been borrowing books on a regular basis. I think he's doing it just to talk to me," she giggled. "He's a widower and will soon retire from the Bromfield Trust Bank."

Veronica told her how pleased she was to hear her news. "He did say something yesterday that was odd, though. It seems the bank had a break-in recently that was kept quiet and out of the papers. The thieves didn't take money; they took a painting from the wall of the conference room that was on loan to the bank from a Boston collector. They left two other paintings by famous artists and only took the one picture. The bank doesn't know what to make of it, and the police have no leads."

Just at that moment, Joe Banks arrived with coffee and croissants. "We're having a little reunion," said Diane. After accepting compliments from Joe on her appearance, Diane recounted the bank incident.

"I'm familiar with the case. I interviewed Giles Gordon of the Artemis Gallery who represented the donor that gifted the bank with the painting that was stolen."

"Do you remember the name of the donor, Joe?" asked Veronica.

"Yes, the painting was from the Hunt Collection."

Veronica and Diane looked at each other and changed the subject.

After Joe left, she ran to the phone and started to dial.

"Tell me you're not calling Harry," cried Diane.

"Why wouldn't he tell me about this and here is another connection between Harry and Giles Gordon. There's something rotten in Denmark and I'm going to get to the bottom of it if it's the last thing I do," quivered Veronica, pushing her harlequin glasses back up her nose.

"That's just it; it just *might* be the very last thing you do. Put the phone down and let's talk about this."

Veronica missed talking to Diane, who had a singularly easy way of cutting through the red tape and getting to the nub of the matter. "You've got to confront Harry with all these questions. You need answers, and he has to come clean. You've been through too much not to be told the whole truth."

Veronica shook her head and whispered half to herself. "I really don't know him at all. Is he a crook, is he a victim, or is he caught in a web of deceit not of his making?"

CHAPTER 15

Summer was now in full-blown mode, and the hot, humid dog days of June kept sales to a minimum on Posy Place. Veronica's Vintage only had fans to cool down the store, and the ice-cream shop next door was doing a rush of business.

The shop's bell tinkled as Sam the mailman delivered the day's mail. The usual bills and junk mail arrived as did a large cream envelope with her name handwritten in formal script. There was only a post office box number as the return address. Veronica distractedly slit open the envelope and was surprised to find an invitation to the Bromfield Yacht Club gala, always held the first Saturday in June, just five days away. She checked again to see that it was addressed to her as she knew no one who belonged to the club. An RSVP envelope slipped out, so she decided to call the number printed on it.

As it turned out, her name was on the invitation list, and she was told it wasn't a mistake. She had been vetted and could bring a guest if she wished. She picked up the phone and called Tom Graham. He would be delighted, he said, to escort her. She spent the rest of the day in a euphoric haze and wondered what she would wear. It seemed so long since she attended a formal affair, and the sheer happiness she felt at being invited surprised her. *I guess I need a happy night out*, she thought.

She assumed that she was invited to the gala because she was a new business owner in town and some of her customers were members of the yacht club. One customer in particular, Linda Simmons, came to the shop on a fairly regular basis, and by coincidence, came in the next day. Linda belonged to many clubs and was a social leader in Bromfield.

"Did you, by any chance, have anything to do with me getting an invitation to the yacht club gala," she asked.

"I honestly had nothing to do with it," said Linda, "but I'm glad I'll see you there. Now, what can I buy that no one else will have on?"

Veronica led her over to a rack of vintage 1980s cocktail dresses and pulled out a short, black-beaded number with power shoulders. Her customer wrinkled her nose and rolled her eyes, but Veronica stood firm and silently pointed a finger toward the dressing room. A few minutes later, a resplendent Linda twirled around and gazed in the mirror. "Yes, just as I thought. You look fabulous; very Joan Collins." She wrapped the package, and another happy customer danced out the door.

Her decision to ask Tom to be her date was in retaliation for all the unanswered questions she had about Harry, the one man she thought she knew. Too many odd things were happening regarding him, and he seemed not to be taking her seriously enough anymore.

Tom, at least, appeared to be forthcoming with information about himself. He had responsibilities to his company and employees and always seemed available to answer her phone calls. She needed a man in her life who was constant and dependable. That man used to be Harry, and she no longer felt the old connection to him. Maybe the night of the dance would reinforce her decision to move on with another man who would turn out to be the right one.

The yacht club dance was the pivotal social event of the summer in Bromfield. Thanks to Linda spreading the news about Veronica's Vintage, several women in town now became steady customers. The stock of clothing and jewelry was depleted daily, and the small pieces of furniture and decorative items were also selling well.

She had her favorite photograph of Aunt Gillian enlarged and framed and hung it in a prominent place in the shop. It became her custom to blow a kiss at the picture every morning when she opened, a homage to her mentor and in loving memory to a life well lived. Gillian was her good luck charm, and sometimes, after a long day, she would stand in front of the photo and talk to her. And sometimes a little thought would pop into her head…and leave as quickly as it came. She chalked it up to Gillian trying to send her advice telepathically. She often asked for advice, and it always seemed to be about Harry. It's almost as if she's telling me not to give up on him, that there's more to Harry than meets the eye. Gillian was always fond of him and told her more than once that he was a man of substance. I've always thought of him that way, but lately, he seems to be another person; as though another being entirely has inhabited his mind and body.

She concluded that maybe Harry was a little jealous now that she was her own boss. After all, has he ever been in a position to be the master of his own fate? As far as she knew, everything that Harry had was handed to him. She couldn't even recall that he had bought any furnishings for his house or even purchased the house, for that matter. As an only child from a wealthy family, he was the sole inheritor of the entire estate, which was considerable.

To be fair, though, she knew he did buy his car, the precious Porsche, his pride and joy. She looked up at Gillian and sighed. "Why is Harry telling me lies? Okay, they are little white lies, but lies, nonetheless. I know you've always told me how lucky I was to have him in my life, but things have changed. Is there something you know that I don't?" She willed the photo to give her answers. She started suddenly as the bell over the front door announced the arrival of a customer.

Later in the day, she put in a call to Harry on his private number. The phone rang several times and then went to voice mail. "Harry, I need to talk to you; please return my call." Later that night she tried calling him again. On the third ring, he answered, but his voice sounded far away.

"Oh, hi, Veronica," he answered nonchalantly. "How are you?"

"Harry, we need to talk. Where are you?"

"Actually I've been out of town the last few days on business and have been meaning to call you. I should be back in Boston tomorrow evening. Can we meet then?"

"I won't be available tomorrow evening," she said coldly. "I have plans."

"What's my girl up to then? You sound quite serious."

"We have to talk about our relationship and the fact that you' been keeping things from me."

The silence on the phone was deafening. "Harry, are you still there?" The phone clicked two times, and the next thing she heard was a dial tone.

"Well, can you beat that," she fumed to the empty room. "He hung up on me!"

That does it, she thought, tears rolling down her cheeks. *I can't believe it's come to this, but I really have to move on. Tom is my future; Harry is my past.* She grabbed some tissues and dabbed her eyes. Then she walked up to Aunt Gillian's picture and said, "Harry fooled you too. And you loved him as much as I do."

Veronica was always a firm believer in retail therapy and trying and buying new beauty products was her way of coping with disappointment. She decided to open the shop a bit late the next morning and marched to her favorite department store, firmly clutching her credit card. The well lit displays of bottles and scents called to her like a siren's song. The saleslady knew a good customer when she saw one and invited her to sit at the counter while she ministered, slathering on creams and potions while keeping up a steady sales patter.

The next stop was at the beauty salon down the street. The owner suggested a new rinse color and a trim. The results were a blue-black gloss and a shorter hairdo, both which were very flattering to her creamy complexion. While there, the manicurist painted her nails a startling shade of crimson. She was delighted with the results and went back to open her shop.

She had decided to wear a 1980s crimson silk chiffon dress that hugged her curves. It had one bare shoulder, and a floaty overlay skirt grazed her ankles when she moved. The strappy, high-heeled sandals showed off her newly painted toenails. *Not bad for a middle-aged woman*, she thought, gazing at her image in the oval cheval mirror. *I wonder what Tom will say when he sees me in this dress.*

She didn't have long to wait for the answer. They had arranged to meet at her shop after closing on Saturday evening. When he walked in looking very handsome in a designer white tuxedo and saw her standing there, all he could say was "Wow," then "Wow" again.

"Do you approve of my new look, sir?" she said, batting her eyelashes.

"I not only approve, but I'm also enchanted," he said and kissed her. "You are a fairy princess, and your coach awaits," he whispered.

She closed the lights and locked the door; then they walked out into the summer night hand in hand.

CHAPTER 16

The weather was perfect, and the warm summer breeze blew softly through Veronica's new hairdo. She felt confident and happy as they entered the main function room of the Bromfield Yacht Club now crowded with couples who greeted one another in cheerful recognition. Many had been members for years, their membership passed down from generation to generation. This dinner dance was a reunion for those who had winter homes in warmer climates who moved back to Massachusetts in the summer.

She recognized many people and her customer, Linda, came up and hugged her. They introduced the men they were with as the society orchestra started playing, adding to the festive mood. Tom was a wonderful dancer, and they enjoyed the bottle of champagne he ordered. The food was delicious, and she was surprised that he knew several people there and identified them as customers for his security business.

The evening was turning out to be wonderful, and when Tom suggested they take a stroll outside to get some fresh air, she agreed and wrapped herself in the white pashmina shawl she brought along. He steered her down to the end of the dock and paused in front of a particularly lovely looking yacht, very sleek in black and white, gleaming in the moonlight. The name of the vessel was in gold lettering on the hull, and she leaned over to read *"Alarming Seas-Boston"*.

"Do you like her?" he asked. She nodded and said, "What is there not to like?" while wondering what to put as a dollar figure on such a magnificent craft.

"I'm so glad because I own her. She's my pride and joy."

"My, you're a dark horse, Tom. Why didn't you tell me you were a member here?"

"I wanted to tell you when you asked me to escort you here tonight, but I thought I would surprise you."

"Well, consider me surprised. Business must be good because this is a luxury item few can afford to own."

"Boats are a weakness of mine," he said with pride. "Ever since I was in the navy, I dreamed of someday doing well enough to own a yacht like this. And here it is, my dream come true."

Suddenly, they felt the start of rain, and by the time they ran back to the ballroom, the skies had opened up, and the weather cooled off quickly. They stood looking out as the water washed over the line of beautiful boats docked outside the function room window. *I'm not going to let a little rain spoil my night*, she thought. In typical New England style, it stopped as quickly as it started.

They went back to their table, where Tom ordered cordials to go with their coffee. The music started up again, and he got up and pulled her on to the dance floor. He was so light on his feet. She couldn't remember the last time she had danced so much.

When the evening was over, Tom offered to drive her back to Boston. He made it clear that he wanted to spend a romantic night at her apartment. For the life of her, she couldn't understand why she didn't want the same. She wasn't being coy because that just wasn't her style; but something told her this wasn't the time. The truth was that she couldn't get Harry out of her head, and she realized that until she did, she couldn't commit to another man, no matter how enticing the thought.

Tom told her he was going to try to break her resolve and kissed her passionately on the lips at her door. The perfect gentleman, she thought, as she put the key in the lock.

On Sunday morning, Veronica had two phone calls to make, one to Mandy and another to Diane. They both wanted full details about her date with Tom. Mandy, never shy about asking about Ronnie's sex life, wanted to know if she spent the night with him. When she heard the hesitation on the phone, she yelped in frustration. Veronica tried to explain she still had feelings for Harry, in spite of herself.

Diane suggested they meet at the bakery, and a cup of hazelnut coffee and a decadent French pastry was just what they both needed. The police had cleared Diane of any involvement in Carl's murder, and she learned they had no leads in his death.

Veronica told her about Tom's yacht and wondered how someone starting a new business could afford such a luxury. "He must be doing better than you thought, or maybe he has a wealthy family, like Harry."

It was then she realized the men had met each other. "Tom said he was going to give Harry a security quote for his house, which is odd because Harry already has installed state-of-the-art everything."

"I would like to be a fly on the wall when those two ever start comparing notes about you," laughed Diane.

"It does seem a coincidence that they have met; also that Harry has met Giles Gordon and then pretended he didn't know him, not to mention that Harry looked for the Arabic on the paper I gave him and knew it was a copy."

"What are you saying?" asked Diane sipping her coffee.

"What I'm saying is that there is a pattern here, and Harry is in the middle of it. And when I tried to corner him to give me some answers, he hung up the phone!"

"Maybe he's involved in something unsavory and is using you as a cover."

"What if it's the other way around, Diane? What if Harry is involved in something serious, and he's trying to keep me out of it?"

The warmth of the bakery and the comforting odors of fresh coffee and sweet dough temporarily halted their conversation. Sunday morning customers started to filter in and place their orders, and the familiar background noises of clinking cutlery and the rattle of cups and saucers lulled them to ponder the reality of their questions. They realized it was hard for them to fathom they were indirectly involved in two murders. They sat quietly sipping coffee and wondered why fate had brought them to this point in their lives.

CHAPTER 17

Business had sufficiently increased at the shop, and she found it necessary to hire a part-time helper. Susan, a high school student at Bromfield High, was the daughter of one of her customers. At odds to find a summer job that didn't involve waiting tables or being a lifeguard, Susan jumped at the chance to work in a shop that sold "cool old things."

One day a man walked in and asked to speak to Veronica. Susan was dusting one of the displays and excused herself to go to the back room and find her. The man handed her his card and asked if there was a quiet place where they could talk. It was almost noon, so she told Susan she could leave a little early for lunch.

The card identified him as Alexander Owen, Special Agent, Federal Bureau of Investigation. She sat at her desk and invited him to take a seat opposite. She saw a short, balding man wearing a conservative brown summer-weight checked suit, a striped yellow tie, and highly polished brown leather shoes with gum soles. He didn't smile as he began to tell her the purpose of his visit.

He was heading up the task force investigating several

stolen pieces of artwork that she was partly responsible for recovering. The members of the ring that stole them were, as she was aware, all deceased—except for the leader, who was still at large. The FBI Regional Office in Boston knew his name, and they were aware that she also knew him.

"Why do you think I know this man?" she asked in wonder.

"Because you have dated him," he replied. "We need your cooperation to bring this criminal to justice, and he is very dangerous. This isn't just a white-collar crime we are talking about here," said Owen, slamming his hand suddenly on the desk. "This man has murdered two people in cold blood and will kill again to get what he wants!"

"Oh my God, Harry," she silently moaned. "What have you done?"

"The Arabic text on that piece of paper is the key," he went on. "It confirms that the two paintings that were stolen match up with our list, and we have a good idea who did the job. He's not quite as clever as he thinks, and this time, we're going to get him."

She was silent while taking in everything he was saying, not wanting to believe it but knowing she had to. Finally, she asked, "What do you expect me to do to help?"

"We are aware there may be some danger involved, and we are prepared to coach you every step of the way. The net is closing in around him. We intend to catch him before he has a chance to murder anyone else.

"And it's only fair to tell you, Miss Howard, the insurance company has posted a substantial reward for the recovery of the missing items."

"Money won't mean much to me if I'm dead," she whispered.

"You are an innocent bystander in all of this, but we know you took some liberties in trying to investigate on your own and may have inadvertently put yourself in harm's way because of your, er, *meddling*, shall we say."

Veronica had the grace to blush. "I was only trying to help a friend who is the ex-wife of one of the thieves."

"Well, we are prepared to turn a blind eye to that little caper; but please, leave the investigation to the professionals from now on. Needless to say, this is an undercover operation, and no word can be leaked. Do I have your promise on that?"

She could only nod her head in the affirmative.

After Special Agent Owen left, she thought about her vow to help Harry. She had just given her word to the FBI that she would help them in any way possible, yet she had given her word to Harry as well. She fought a silent battle with herself. All bets had to be off because Harry was now a known killer to the Bureau, and they were going to catch him and put him in jail for life—or worse—for his actions.

She still couldn't believe he was capable of murder; yet, she heard it with her own ears just a few minutes ago. She knew people could become so obsessed with cravings to own things that all reason left them.

She never thought Harry could ever hurt her physically; yet, he did strike her and then tell her a silly story about a masked man pointing a gun at her. She had so many questions about his lies, silly lies, really, about his knowing Giles Gordon and his secret meetings that he denied having. She realized he had never explained any of these things to her, and worse, he pointedly avoided answering her questions.

The time had come for Veronica to face the facts. She didn't know Harry Hunt at all, at least, the Harry that she was in love with. There! She said it! She was in love with him.

"How could I not see the signs that pointed to the change that has come over him these past few months?" she asked herself. "When did he stop being the happy-go-lucky guy that I am in love with?

"And now I have to help the FBI catch him and put him in prison for life—or even the possibility of a death sentence."

CHAPTER 18

She was aware that the knowledge of Harry's secret could not go further than herself, and her life depended upon that. She was now placed in a position of trust by the Federal Bureau of Investigation, no less, and it was painful not to be able to share this information with Diane, Mandy, or even Joe Banks. She was placed in a position of divided loyalty; yet, she was putting her life in danger to help the police and the FBI catch Harry and bring him to justice for the crimes he has committed just to get his hands on a couple of oil paintings for his collection. She became depressed, and those around her thought she was going through a temporary funk. She felt like a lamb going to the slaughter and knew there was nothing she could do about it.

Agent Owen called and asked her to come to the Regional Office in Boston to talk to two of his operatives working on the case. Agents Leslie Graves and Stephen Gore were kind but firm as they discussed their strategy to catch Harry. She filled her paper cup twice with coffee she couldn't taste, and when Gore left the room temporarily, the younger woman moved over to his chair, reached over to her, and took both her hands and squeezed them. Veronica started to cry in spite of herself.

"Look, I know this is hard for you; we all realize that. To tell the truth, if it were my boyfriend that was involved, I'd go to pieces," she said handing her a box of tissues.

The green painted room felt as if it were closing in on her as she looked down at her lap. Why do all these official offices look the same? she wondered. I could be sitting in the interrogation room at Bromfield Police Headquarters, in the same gray metal chair, at the same gray metal table, drinking the same awful coffee. She blinked and realized her mind was wandering.

"I know you're trying to be kind, but it's not your boyfriend, it's mine, and I'm trying to wrap my mind around this entire nightmare."

Neither woman said anything for a few minutes until Agent Gore came back to the room holding a sheaf of papers and a small electronic device. The plan was to bug her apartment and store telephones, and when Harry called, she would request that he meet her at a location of their choosing. During that meeting, she would be wearing the device he held up to record the conversation. They were interested to know the details of his movements during the next few weeks.

"We know how hard this is for you," said Leslie, "but it's your duty to help us bring this man to justice."

All she could do was to nod her head before reaching for more tissues.

The week dragged by, and she found it hard to be enthusiastic about anything. One of her best customers came in one day and observed her flagging spirits and asked if she was feeling all right. She realized she couldn't continue to mope around and set about cleaning the store, scrubbing the floor, washing the windows—anything to keep busy. Susan asked if she was feeling unwell and took the spray bottle from her hands and finished wiping down the dressing room mirrors.

That afternoon Tom called. He explained he had been away on a business trip and just got back. His upbeat voice and mood were perfect, and when he suggested an outing Sunday afternoon to show her his new yacht, she jumped at the idea. A diversion was just what she needed right now. She said she would pack a hamper of food if he would bring the wine.

The weather forecast for Sunday was for a partly cloudy but warm afternoon. She decided to wear navy slacks and a nautical-themed sweater of red and navy with a sailor collar. Her red boat shoes matched her lipstick and nail polish. She realized for the first time in weeks she was smiling. Tom picked her up, and they drove to the yacht club which was crowded with families eager to enjoy the calm and tranquil sea. The flags on the dock fluttered occasionally, and the festive atmosphere was punctuated with the plaintive cries of seagulls perched on the pilings hoping for someone to throw them food.

Ronnie packed the hamper with cold roast chicken, her

special homemade pâté, deviled eggs, and potato salad. She brought a decadent double chocolate cake from the bakery and filled a thermos with hot coffee. They walked down the ramp together presenting a picture of a happy couple looking forward to an anticipated outing on a beautiful summer day. They continued to walk past boats of every description, each getting larger and more elaborate until they finally stopped in front of the *Alarming Seas*. She remembered her surprise when she first saw it at the night of the gala.

"Wow," she said, her eyes taking in the size.

"I never do anything in a small way, Ronnie," he laughed. "It's always go big or go home for me."

They climbed aboard, and Tom gave her a tour of the wheelhouse and the sophisticated sonar equipment that he was particularly proud of. They went below, and he pointed out the boat sleeps four. He had already used it for a business outing for some of his best clients. *They must have been as impressed as I am*, she thought, noting the quality of the decorations.

One particularly nice touch was a beautifully painted seascape hanging in the salon. She took her harlequin glasses out of her bag and peered closely at the signature while Tom told her it was a nineteenth-century Dutch oil on canvas. She noted the spacious galley and the set of dishes, each decorated with an intricate sailor's knot in blue and gold and the words, "Alarming Seas."

I could get used to this, she thought. Life with Tom would be comfortable and free of angst. He must be doing well in his business, and he genuinely seems to care for me, or at the very least, we have a strong mutual attraction. Suddenly, she blushed deeply, realizing her premature assumption, and that she was probably one of many women that Tom Graham dated.

She set out unpacking the hamper, and they decided to eat after about half an hour out of the confines of the yacht club. They sat out on the deck, drinking in the sea air and sun along with the chardonnay that Tom provided. He had a small chilled wine cabinet installed in the galley filled with mostly vintage years. She glanced at him out of the corner of her eye. *He has it all,* she thought, *and the class to know that you don't have to steal anything to be happy.* She sighed deeply and sipped her wine, content with the lazy day and grateful that her companion was as happy as she was.

They talked about the advertising business, and, of course, Mandy's name came up. Tom admitted that he sent her a large bouquet of flowers to thank her for suggesting he call her for a date. They both laughed when Veronica admitted to doing the same. "Her office must look like a florist's shop," she said, happy with the thought that he was a gentleman.

Suddenly, a squall blew up, and they decided to go back to port. She snuggled next to him as he maneuvered the big boat back to the slip. The wind was now blowing in sharp gusts as they dashed from the dock to the dining room bar.

"I think we need a drink," he said and ordered two

martinis. They sat happily chatting with the other patrons when the bartender told Tom he was wanted on the house phone. "I wonder who that is," he said and disappeared to the next room. When he returned, he said he had to stay and talk to the manager about a security problem the club was experiencing.

"Do you mind if I don't drive you back to Boston?" As she had her car in the parking lot where she met him that morning, she said it wasn't a problem. He promised to call her soon. She was a little tired after the outing and knew she had to meet the FBI team in the morning before she opened the shop. They kissed good-bye, and she left.

CHAPTER 19

Veronica arrived a few minutes early for her appointment at the FBI Regional Office and was ushered in and given a cup of coffee. The three-person task team assigned to the case filed in. Agent Leslie Graves greeted her with a small smile, and Agent Stephen Gore shook her hand. Both were somberly dressed in gray. *They're dressed to match the tables and chairs*, she thought, trying to bring a little levity to the day.

The room was set up with a large whiteboard bearing photos of the late Carl Andrews and Patch and other pictures of the crime scene. Special Agent Owen was the last to arrive and walked over to the board. *Does the man ever smile?* she wondered, as he picked up a baton and pointed to the photo of Patch. He revealed that Patch was the liaison that provided the chief suspect with leads to the houses they robbed. The Bureau was watching another person who also was suspected of doing the same.

"That wouldn't be Giles Gordon, by any chance?" she asked. Three sets of eyebrows shot up, and Owen asked what she knew about him. She explained she always had a feeling he wasn't entirely what he seemed to be and recounted her dealings with him.

Owen put down the baton and took a seat. "We've had Gordon and the Artemis Gallery under surveillance for some time now. He's in a perfect position to know where, what, and how works of art are positioned, and we believe he was the fence for several of the pieces that were stolen. Under the guise of a respectable businessman, he finds out who owns what paintings, what they are insured for, and where they are located. He then informs his customer, who then places an order for the pieces he wants to have stolen. A nice little setup.

"We also believe Patch was his employee and go-between. At some point, Patch held out on some information as a double cross, or he tried to cut out Gordon altogether, and the chief suspect stabbed him and dumped his body in the harbor."

Veronica shuddered and tried to block out that picture from her mind.

Owen continued. "We've had our inside man on this case for over a year now and have almost enough proof to make the arrest. He will be joining us shortly to fill you in."

Agent Gore spoke. "With the cooperation of the Bromfield Police Department and the Massachusetts State Police, we now believe we can tighten the net around our chief suspect and need just one more piece to the puzzle before we can make an arrest. Over to you, Leslie."

Agent Graves picked up the baton and pointed to the photo of Carl Andrews. "We are aware that you and Mrs.

Andrews found his body in the abandoned house, and that the evidence was obtained from the safe on the property. The information that was contained on the paper written in Arabic pointed us to our chief suspect, and we are grateful to you for turning it over to the local police."

A knock on the door interrupted and heralded the arrival of the other agent on the case, and Veronica turned around in her chair to face a smiling Harry.

"I believe you know Special Agent Hunt," said Owen.

Veronica leaped up from the chair and flung her arms around Harry, burying her head in his chest, tears of relief rolling down her face.

Another box of tissues on the table was pushed at her as she sat down again and blew her nose.

"I have a lot to explain to you later," said Harry, "but right now, we have a criminal to catch and only you can lead us to him."

"But I don't know who you mean," she spluttered, trying to take in what she was hearing.

"Oh yes, you do," said Owen. "Spencer T. Stewart, Paul Stephen Thomas, T. Kenneth Parsons...These are only a few of his aliases. But you know him as Tom Graham."

Her mouth flew open, but nothing came out.

"It's not often my girl is caught off guard and speechless," joked Harry. "But seriously, Graham is the major player in an international stolen art ring, and I've been tracking him for the better part of a year now. His greed has driven him to murder two people that we know of and perhaps more."

Owen held up his thumb and forefinger a half inch apart. "We are *this* close to catching him, and with your help, we will."

"But what can I do?"

Owen walked around to the front of her chair and put his hand on her shoulder. "You can continue to see him socially and feed us information. We want to set up a sting that will nail this guy once and for all. We will fit you with a wire for that purpose."

Ronnie thought a minute, shaking her head to clear it. "You mean you want to use me as bait."

"I wouldn't put it that way, Miss Howard," said Owen, tugging his earlobe.

"How *would* you put it?" she asked and turned to Harry for the answer.

He sat down beside her, took her hands in his, and said, "This is the part I hate." He looked around at the three agents and continued. "I know what's at stake here better than anyone. This guy kills on a whim to get what he wants. He's a dangerous psychopath, and his greed knows no bounds. He has ruined lives and families and will continue to do so for as long as we let him.

"Right now, he thinks he's setting me up to steal my paintings, family heirlooms that are in my keeping that generations have enjoyed. Many are on loan to museums so that others can enjoy them. But under the guise of a 'security consultant,' he wants to steal them for himself. I can't let that happen."

Harry continued. "You know I've been playing a cat-and-mouse game with him for months now, playing hard to get, not returning his phone calls, and cancelling appointments. I believe he mentioned this to you on one of your dates."

Veronica looked down and blushed.

"Graham is aware of the net worth of my pictures and knows he will never be able to exhibit them except in his own house behind locked doors. But he wants them; wants them badly."

Owen spoke up. "We can't think of any other way to catch this guy without involving you directly. It will set us back at least a year if we don't act now with you to help us. He doesn't suspect you, and you're the only one with direct access to him. We need to keep up the charade of your estrangement from Harry as it is a perfect cover for us. You're the only one that can do this."

She sighed, opened her pocketbook, took out her cosmetic case and searched for her red lipstick. With all eyes on her, she applied it and snapped the case shut. "No pressure at all," she murmured. She looked into Harry's pleading eyes, and her heart melted. "I'll do it for you; you know I will."

They stared at each other, and neither heard the round of applause.

CHAPTER 20

Trust had to be re-established, and there was so much to explain. The FBI recruited Harry through a friend who realized he had the perfect cover. His family name, background as a collector, and reputation as a wealthy man who didn't need to work was all advantageous. He would be perceived by art thieves as a mark, and not a very intelligent one at that. The life of an undercover agent is dangerous and lonely, he explained, and many times he was close to taking her into his confidence before he realized he would be placing her in great danger.

One of the reasons he accepted the job was that he took the position of caretaker for his family's heritage very seriously. The thought that a thief could come along and steal what took decades, and in some cases, centuries, to collect and conserve made his blood boil. The Hunt Family Foundation loaned paintings to both the public and private sector, to museums, and municipal buildings, for everyone to enjoy. Some of the most storied names in American art were represented in the collection, and he oversaw the task of funding, upkeep, and security of these treasures. Even Veronica was unaware of his art education background, which included advanced degrees in security analysis, conservation techniques, and Interpol training.

She realized more than ever that Harry was an exceptionally intelligent and driven man who worked hard at presenting to the world a very different picture. His easygoing nature worked in his favor to throw these thieves off their stride.

He explained he had the conflict to face of his feelings for her versus allowing her to be placed in danger on this job. Several times, he retreated to collect his thoughts and never called her back because he had to tell her several lies to continue his cover. Putting her in harm's way was the last thing he wanted to do.

"So much for that idea," he said and smiled ruefully. "Now it looks like you will be doing just what I didn't want to happen. When I saw you were getting close to Graham, it tore me up. I saw my lovely girl drifting away, and that bastard moving in. Now he's going to get what he deserves."

"I have so many questions, Harry. What about the night in the restaurant parking lot when you hit me? Was someone really going to shoot me?"

"Yes. There was someone with a gun and a mask, and I'm pretty sure it was Giles Gordon. We now know he is a major fence for stolen artwork and is the supply line for Graham. He legitimately bids on paintings at auctions on Graham's behalf, but he also knows who owns valuable pictures worth stealing. We can also tie him in to past museum robberies as an accessory, including one very publicized heist here in Boston.

"I put myself forth as a private investor in the Artemis Gallery to keep an eye on him. My card you saw on his desk that day was a million-in-one mistake. "Keeping a low profile is very important for these people. Gordon must have thought you overheard something at his gallery and didn't want to take any chances, so he tried to silence you in an attempted mugging. My hitting and pushing you probably saved your life, but it hurt me to do it to you."

"Oh, Harry," she cried. "I can't begin to tell you how sorry I am that I doubted you. I'll do anything now to help put Tom Graham behind bars."

The sting operation was already in place. Veronica had to pretend she and Harry were still at odds and resume her life at the store. It was hard for her to keep her mind on her work, but she knew Harry's life depended on her playing this dangerous game with conviction. She also knew her life would be in danger if she made a false move. Graham was a clever career criminal with no conscience. He had murdered to get what he wanted.

Harry was to be the pivot man and her coach. The plan was that she would wear a hidden microphone, and they decided that Veronica's Vintage was the safest place to meet. It was her task to lure Graham there. Could she keep up the charade of finding him attractive and act as if nothing had changed since last week? she wondered. *How can I flirt with this monster and pretend he is the new man in my life now that I know how evil he really is?*

She had to sit and wait for Graham to call. It was hard for her to concentrate on shop business, and she relied on Susan, her helper, to deal with the mundane tasks of running the store. The Bureau cautioned her not to change her daily routine or do anything that would cast suspicion on her activities. She still couldn't reveal anything to Diane or even to Joe Banks.

Under the guise of repairing a broken air conditioner, a team of security experts came to the store to install electronic devices. Everything had to appear as normal, and she found it nerve-racking every time the phone rang. She remembered that not too many months ago, she wanted to be Mata Hari in her daydreams. Now that the idea was not so preposterous, she was sorry the thought ever crossed her mind. The old saying, "Be careful what you wish for" had become very real to her.

She had to pretend she no longer had feelings for Harry when all she wanted to do was hold him close and tell him in her heart she never stopped loving him. When Mandy called to ask how things were going with Tom, she had all she could do to not gnash her teeth and not tell her the man she thought would be perfect for her was a cold-blooded murderer. It seemed that Tom Graham, or whatever his real name was, had everyone fooled...well, almost everyone.

Veronica was as close to giving things away as ever when both Diane and Joe came to the store one morning. She was keeping up the pretense that everything was normal when

Harry's name came up. She automatically smiled, then giggled, then remembered she was supposed to have broken up with him. She quickly turned her giggle into a sob and turned her head, hoping they interpreted her actions as feelings of regret. It was hard hiding your feelings from friends, she thought, wishing she was anywhere else on the planet.

CHAPTER 21

The call finally came three days later on a bright and warm summer morning. The shop wasn't particularly busy, and the stock of vintage woven hats with wide brims and the window display of raffia straw tote bags along with other summertime items had been depleted days ago. Veronica was busy at her desk catching up on paperwork when Susan told her she was wanted on the phone.

"Hi, there, sunshine," chirped Tom. "It's a perfect day for a little cruise on my boat. Can I entice you to close up shop and come out with me?"

What a smug jerk, she thought. *He thinks he has the world by the tail, but we'll see about that. I'm committed to bringing him down, and it will be a pleasure to see him put away for all the misery and devastation he has caused.* Still, her hand was shaking as she held the phone and forced herself to be upbeat.

"What a nice surprise. Why don't you come here instead, and we can bring a picnic to the beach," she countered, knowing that particular scenario was what the FBI would prefer.

"The water is just right, and the boat will give us some

privacy. There are a couple of things I want to discuss with you, and I would rather do it from the privacy of my boat. Meet me at the yacht club at noon and bring a bathing suit." He hung up before she could answer.

She panicked and immediately called Harry.

"It's not ideal," he said, "but we may not get another chance so soon." He put her on hold, then came back on the line.

"That was Owen. They heard the call on the phone bug and agree that we should go ahead with Graham's request.

"Here's the plan. The woman agent you have met, Leslie Graves, will come to the shop in about half an hour posing as a customer and will try on some clothing in the dressing room. You will assist her. She will fit you with a hidden microphone. When you're ready, close the shop and meet Graham at the yacht club as he requested. Try to stall and keep him from taking the boat out of the slip. Undercover agents will be waiting to board and arrest him. Do you have any questions?"

"But, Harry, what if I can't stop him from sailing?"

"Don't worry; there is a Plan B. Go along with him if he wants to leave the harbor. If there is any sign of trouble—any word from him that he is suspicious—don't argue or fight him. Just lie and tell him he's mistaken. We will hear everything you say and act accordingly. Just be yourself, my darling, and everything will be all right."

Harry's soothing words didn't really stop her heart from racing. She knew the whole operation depended upon her keeping a cool head. Any slipup and it could put her life in danger. *Why did I agree to go along with this?* she asked herself for the hundredth time. She answered as promptly as she asked. *Because this guy thinks he can manipulate the man I love and me, that's why.* Her feisty resolve was coming through, and there was no stopping herself now.

Agent Graves came in the shop a short time later asking to see some dresses in her size. The show had begun. Susan waited on another customer while she took the agent to a dressing room and was fitted with a specially hidden microphone.

"How are you feeling?" she asked.

"I'm a nervous wreck, but I'm going through with this, no matter what."

"You're doing just fine. Stick to the plan and don't try to be a hero. Play into his plans, and we'll be there for you with the safety net."

"I just don't want to mess up, Leslie."

"Don't worry; you won't. You want to get this guy just as much as we do. Think of it as Girl Power!"

They both giggled, then, and it broke the ice, but they were aware of the enormous risk Veronica was taking.

It was almost noon when she drove into the yacht club parking lot. She opened her trunk and took out the hamper of food that she had prepared. The walk down the jetty out to Tom's yacht was the same route she had taken just over a week ago, but a world away from the circumstances that brought her here today. A week ago, she was hopeful and carefree, spending the day with a new man she thought was charming and exciting. Now, she knew he was a thief and a killer, and it was all she could do to force sincerity in her eyes and a smile on her lips. She would try to focus on the task of helping the authorities put him away. *I must have been mad to think he was better than Harry*, she thought once again.

Tom was standing at the end of the dock watching her walk toward him with a huge grin on his face. *Look at him*, she thought, *so sure that he is going to continue on his merry way without any consequences. How could I have ever been deceived by his smile, and why was I dazzled by his manners and ego? I guess I just have to give Graham his due and admit that he is an expert in deceiving people. That's probably why they call them confidence tricksters; con men. Yes, I'm looking at the poster boy for a con man.*

She plastered on a smile that she hoped was sincere as he walked up and kissed her on the cheek and took the hamper and a tote bag from her.

"Why don't you change into your bathing suit?" he suggested, untying the ropes from the metal rings on the dock.

Because I'm wearing a wire, she thought. "I'll wait until we are underway," and she continued to empty the hamper in the galley.

He skillfully maneuvered the yacht from the slip into the harbor, and the steady hum of the twin screw motors kept her focused. A warm breeze was blowing, and the day promised perfect weather. She breathed the salt air deeply into her lungs as she joined him next to the wheel. He had made up a cocktail shaker of martinis, and they nibbled on the cheese and crackers she had brought. Several other yachts sailed by, and they waved gaily at the occupants while he held on to the wheel with one hand and her waist with the other.

They presented a picture of perfect harmony and bliss to anyone who saw them. After about a half hour, she decided to go below and unpack lunch. She walked around the salon and wanted to look again at the Dutch painting that she had admired on the first visit. Why does this seem so familiar to me? she wondered. Then it hit her. This was the painting described in Arabic that was stolen from the Castle Hill estate in the robbery that Carl and Patch were involved in—and ultimately died over.

She tried to control her shaking hands by shoving them in the pockets of the navy-blue nautical sweater she was wearing and failed to notice that Tom had walked up behind her and was watching her closely.

She turned around and smiled. "What did you want to discuss with me, Tom? You mentioned something on the phone this morning."

He ignored her question. "You seem to like this nice print of an old nautical painting."

"Oh, it doesn't look like a print," she blurted out and realized too late her mistake. Why didn't she ever notice his smile showed pointed teeth like a wolf's?

"Actually, it isn't a print but a nineteenth-century Dutch

oil on canvas, as I mentioned to you before."

"Oh, you know me," she recovered. "I don't know an original from a print." She laughed trying to cover her gaffe. *Maybe if I pretend I'm an airhead, he won't notice my mistake*, she thought.

"Now that's not entirely true, is it?" he leered. "I think you do know the difference quite well. At least that's what Giles Gordon tells me. You went to his gallery with family photos of some oils you wanted to be appraised. He remembers you well, especially after you returned with your boyfriend, Harry Hunt."

The hair on Veronica's neck stood up, but she was determined to act as if nothing could rattle her. "Oh, do you know Mr. Gordon too?" she asked, flipping her hand in dismissal.

Out of the corner of her eye she caught sight of the knife she was using to cut the cheese she brought. She started to walk toward the galley when he caught her around the waist and pulled her toward him.

"Let's stop pretending you don't know who I am or what I do, shall we?" he growled, pulling at her arm with a sharp wrench.

"Tom, I don't know what you mean," she cried, trying to wriggle out of his grasp. He was hurting her now, and his eyes held a manic glow.

She tried to break free, but he wouldn't let her go. "What's gotten in to you, Tom? Let me go."

"Here's what I wanted to tell you, my dear Veronica," he sneered. "I know Hunt is on to me, and I'm also aware you know I run a syndicate that steals valuable artwork. There's no way I can allow you to leave this boat alive. You will have an 'accident,' fall overboard, and I, unfortunately, will be unable to save you."

She screamed then, realizing the reality of what he was saying.

"No one can hear you, dear Ronnie, so save your breath. I'll be out of the country by tonight, and you will be dead."

He then tried to frog march her toward the stairs. She kicked backward as hard as she could, catching his leg. He yelped out in pain and tightened his grip on her arm and twisted her forward. The wire she was wearing became detached and exposed in the struggle. He saw it and pulled it away from her body yelling, "What's this?" and threw her against a glass table. She landed hard on the floor, dazed and sore and unable to get up on her own.

He ran up the stairs to the pilot house, shoved the gears ahead, and headed out to sea. It was then he heard the helicopter hovering overhead and saw the gray Coast Guard cutter at starboard.

"You are surrounded and cannot escape," commanded the voice on the loudspeaker. "Prepare to be boarded."

Graham wasn't about to be intimidated. He ran back downstairs to Ronnie and roughly propped her on her feet. He saw the knife in the galley and tried to reach it.

I'm not going down without a fight, she thought and had the presence of mind to elbow him quickly. She turned around and raked her crimson nails down his cheeks, causing him to loosen his grip. Then she ran to the coffee table, picked up a heavy crystal ashtray, and banged him over the head with it with all her might. He slid to the floor, out cold.

She was dazed and hurt and starting to feel faint when she saw Coast Guard uniforms rush into the salon, quickly followed by Special Agents Owen, Gore, and Hunt. Harry hugged her tenderly and whispered, "We've got him, thanks to my brave girl wearing a not-so-hidden microphone."

CHAPTER 22

Harry insisted on taking Veronica to the hospital to have the doctors assess her injuries. She left with her arm in a sling, an ankle bandage, and painkillers in her system. She was bruised and sore but happy to be alive and safe again at home. Harry made her tea, and they sat on her blue velvet sofa hugging each other for dear life.

"When Graham started to push you around, I thought I was going to lose my mind. It made me realize more than ever that I can never be without you, Veronica."

"I didn't know what to think, and I was hurt and unhappy because of all the lies and stories you told me, and I thought you didn't love me any longer," she sniffed.

He kissed her tenderly and gazed in her eyes. "I couldn't reveal my real profession to you. You understand that now, don't you, my darling? I've had the perfect cover for several years now, and I take my work seriously. Don't think I've not come close to telling you several times, but it was always better for me that you thought I was just a wealthy dilettante rather than a dedicated law enforcement officer because that's what I am."

After a few days of well-earned rest, Veronica was back

at the store, happy to be alive and very happy to return to her life. Agent Owen informed her that the reward offered by the insurance company for the return of the Dutch painting was hers. She proudly displayed the FBI Commendation she received at a special ceremony at their Boston office on the wall behind her desk. She was featured in several news stories and was called as the chief witness for the prosecution at the trial of Tom Graham for murder and grand theft.

Diane and Amanda met for the first time at the Welcome Home party Harry hosted at the shop, and Joe Banks smiled like a proud father every time Veronica looked his way. He looked different out of his uniform, and the cold beer he clutched helped him cool down on that warm evening. The local Thai restaurant catered at Veronica's request, and a bar was set up in a corner on her desk. It was a happy occasion, and many of the local shop owners attended, congratulating her on her bravery and intelligence. It seemed to hit home finally that her life was happy, and she was content. She had a man she loved and who loved her back, her business was working out very well, and she was doing what she always wanted to do.

During the evening, Veronica insisted Diane accept an envelope containing half of the reward money for her part in Graham's ultimate arrest. Mandy took her aside and told her how jealous she was of her friend because her life was so complete.

She decided to close the store for a few days after the party and take a well-earned vacation. The night before,

Harry came to help her pack some belongings. She took him by the hand and walked over to Aunt Gillian's picture, and they stood silently gazing up at it.

After a while, Veronica said, "She always liked you, you know."

He laughed. "I knew that woman had excellent taste!"

"You have no idea," she said and kissed him before he could say anything else.

Lightning Source UK Ltd.
Milton Keynes UK
UKHW012211141120
373401UK00001B/149